Blind Justice is extremely well written. All of the stories were very gripping and the plots were easy to follow. The stories are memorable and very enjoyable, which gives the reader a fondness for the characters. Being blind myself, I feel the author has a very good grasp of the life of a blind person.

Craig West, BA in Music
Professional Musician
Totally blind from birth

Blind Justice, featuring sight-impaired people, thoroughly delighted me. I think these stories would be especially interesting to visually-impaired teenagers as they cope with their ever expanding world. These stories will entertain and inspire any vision-impaired person and be entertaining and educational for the sighted as they recognize the ways of the blind.

Sylvia Paxton
Blind Professional Musician

I found the short stories in *Blind Justice* unique and entertaining. I also enjoyed seeing the pleasure that they gave to my visually impaired husband.

Isabel Flemons
CHN (Community Health Nurse), retired

BLIND JUSTICE

Short Stories about the Visually Impaired

Lyn Thompson

LYN THOMPSON

BLIND JUSTICE
Copyright © 2014 by Lyn Thompson

ISBN: 978-1-4866-0602-3

Word Alive Press
131 Cordite Road, Winnipeg, MB R3W 1S1
www.wordalivepress.ca

WORD ALIVE
—P R E S S—

Library and Archives Canada Cataloguing in Publication

Thompson, Lyn, Author
     Blind justice / Lyn Thompson.

Short stories.
ISBN 978-1-4866-0602-3 (pbk.).--ISBN 978-1-4866-0603-0 (pdf).--
ISBN 978-1-4866-0604-7 (html).--ISBN 978-1-4866-0605-4 (epub)

     I. Title.

PS8639.H628B55 2014   C813'.6   C2014-905761-X
                                              C2014-905762-8

This book of short stories was written especially for the sight-impaired and the sighted who care to read them aloud to their blind friends or read them for their own enjoyment.

CONTENTS

INTRODUCTION

This book of short stories was written for and is dedicated to the late Coralie Arthur, who said one day, "Why doesn't anyone write stories about blind heroines who have done something special?" Lyn took up the challenge and wrote her first story, "Blind Justice," from the perspective of a blind person and her guide dog.

For sighted readers, Lyn explains that the stories portray the four senses hearing, taste, touch, and smell but, of course, not sight. That is why it is suggested that if you have sighted listeners, they close their eyes to listen as you read. For the sighted, closing their eyes will enhance their perception of the other four senses at work in the stories.

Upon Lyn's request, Coralie named the heroine and the dog. She chose the names Lillian for the heroine and Pickwick for the guide dog. She checked the stories to be sure that Lillian and Pickwick were portrayed accurately according to her own perceived possible abilities. The author, Lyn Thompson, thanks Craig West, Sylvia Paxton, and Roger Woodgate, all vision impaired, for their examination and approval of the portrayal of Lillian in these stories.

Now, meet your super heroine, Lillian, and her dog, Pickwick.

BLIND JUSTICE

I

"There's too much traffic here, Pickwick. Take me to a sidewalk." A car honks at the middle-age woman and her black lab guide dog. "Exhaust fumes—we must be in the parking lot. Find the stores, Pickwick, before we get run over. Pickwick, straight! Straight to the sidewalk!"

The dog winds in and out around parked cars with Lillian hanging on to the stiff handle of his harness. Finally, she feels him step up. The smell of dry cleaning wafts through the air, and Lillian knows they have reached the first shop on the sidewalk that runs past the stores at the mall. "We made it, Pickwick—all the way to the shopping centre on our first try! I think Harold will be pleased with our adventure, providing you don't tell him we got lost in the parking lot. But then, you and Harold don't talk to each other much, so our secret should be safe."

Lillian always talks to her black lab as if he were human, for he seems to understand everything. Her husband, Harold, has always admired his wife's determination, but now that she has Pickwick, he shudders at some of her exploits. There seems to be nothing she won't dare.

"Pickwick, straight. Mimi's Muffin Shop is this way."

With the warm days of summer, there are many customers passing through store entrances, making it easy for Lillian's nose or ears to recognize each shop. She knows the mall from shopping with her husband. The next door has the fragrance of perfume mixed with the odour of chemicals. This marks the beauty parlour. Then she hears the sounds of electronic games, followed by the unmistakable scent of new shoes. Lillian and Pickwick continue on until the aroma of fresh baking floats on the air.

"Here we are, Pickwick. It's time for our treat." She urges the dog to lead her into Mimi's Muffin Shop.

Pickwick goes first to the order counter and waits while Lillian collects her coffee and muffin and pays the bill. Next, he leads her to an empty table. While she starts on her blueberry muffin, he sits at her feet, enjoying his Milk-Bone.

Lillian listens for the rustle of other customers but hears no one over the background music. A few pass on the street, and the clerk moves around at her work, but there is no chatter at the other tables. Such a pity, she thinks, for she does so enjoy eavesdropping.

After the last crumb of muffin disappears, Lillian listens to her watch. Only ten thirty—she has lots of time to visit other stores and be home for her husband's phone call that comes every day at noon.

"Pickwick, let's go to the washroom before we leave." He leads her down the narrow hallway at the back of the shop— first door, "Men," second door, "Ladies."

As she and Pickwick emerge from the washroom, she hears boots thumping down the hall towards her.

"Out of my way, you old blind bat!" comes a rough voice.

Lillian flattens herself to the wall as the man pushes himself past. The boots continue to run to the rear of the shop. A door slams, followed by silence, except for a low growl from Pickwick that blends with the soft music of the restaurant.

"Some people can be so rude, Pickwick. I'm not surprised that you didn't like him very much."

Lillian and Pickwick return to the front area. Pickwick leads Lillian directly across the room to the front door.

"Goodbye, until next time," she says sweetly towards the order desk as she passes on her way to the street. The clerk does not reply.

Window-shopping at the craft store does not interest Lillian as it might others. They walk on and enter the drugstore. Within minutes, she hears sirens wailing outside. At the checkout counter she enquires if the sirens brought police, firemen, or ambulance attendants.

"Can't say for sure, ma'am," a young woman's voice answers. "The last customer said that someone just robbed Mimi's Muffin Shop—must have pushed the clerk so hard she fell and bumped her head. I'd go and have a look for you but I have to stay at the pharmacy till."

"Oh dear, Pickwick. Do you think that man who rushed past us in the corridor robbed Mimi's? Let's go and see what's happening."

"See? Really?" says the clerk. "I thought you couldn't see."

Lillian doesn't answer, for she and Pickwick are already at the door.

Instead, she says to Pickwick as they hustle towards Mimi's, "Why can't people realize that the blind conjure up their own images from sounds and aromas and feel that they've 'seen' something?"

⁓

"Officer, could I have a word with you?"

"I'm rather busy, ma'am. Ask at the shop next door if you need help."

"No, no, you don't understand. I just came out of Mimi's. Perhaps I can help with your investigation."

After what Lillian thinks is a long pause, the officer offers a kindly, "It's okay, ma'am. You and your dog can go on your way. I think we'll find enough evidence to solve the crime. Thanks anyway."

Irritated by the policeman's disbelief in the blind, Lillian starts to retrace her steps towards home, following Pickwick's lead. After completing the route through the parking lot, which still remains a mystery to Lillian, they stand at the intersection with lights. When the traffic halts, Pickwick crosses the road and moves off to the left. At the juniper hedge, Lillian urges the dog into a right turn. They continue on for three blocks, and with the smell of lilacs, they turn into Lillian's driveway, well in time for Harold's phone call.

⁓

"And do you know, Harold, the policeman didn't even ask for my name and address when I offered to help," she ends her story.

"He likely needs a witness who can identify the thief and didn't expect a middle-age lady with a guide dog to be much help," says Harold. "What were you doing at the mall anyway?"

"Trying to see if I could get there, what else?" She laughs. "And we did! My world just grew five blocks bigger. You can't stop us from trying. You have no idea how pleasant I find my kind of view along those streets. What with the wind in the trees, the birds, the fragrance of flowers, and the swish of water sprinklers, it makes for a lovely stroll."

The next day, Lillian and Pickwick head for the mall again. After the lilacs, she turns east as before, with the sun on her face. The warmth on her cheeks reminds her of her faint childhood memories of the lush green of lawns and trees and the brown tones of tree trunks, all highlighted by the dancing sun. She feels sorry for the blind people who have never been able to see anything. Eternally grateful that she can imagine colour, in her mind she designs beautiful landscaping for every home according to the scents of flowers and shrubs that she passes.

When they arrive at Mimi's, Pickwick does not enter. With urging to go forward, he sits at her feet.

"You can't go in today, lady," a passerby explains. "It's closed temporarily. Police business. Seems the waitress died in hospital from bumping her head."

Lillian puts her ear to the display window. The police are inside. She bangs on the door, determined to offer her help.

An officer opens it a crack. "You can't have coffee here today, ma'am. Sorry. Try the restaurant at the other end of the mall," and the door slips shut in her face.

"But I want to help," she shouts at the plate glass. No one returns to hear her out.

For the next few days Lillian tries to forget Mimi's Muffin Shop, but the harder she tries, the more she is convinced that she must go to the police. She knows more about the murderer than anyone. Memories stay strong when you're accosted.

"Harold, take me to the police station. I must make them understand that I can help."

The officer on duty takes her name and address and listens to her story.

"So he had on heavy boots with steel taps on the toes and smelled of mechanic's grease. You know as well as I, ma'am, that many men fit that description. Even if you say that the killer stood six feet tall because you heard his voice from above your head and that he smoked pot and chewed spearmint gum to hide his bad breath, a jury isn't going to convict a man for life on that evidence. Juries want a witness who saw something. Anyway, I understand they've arrested a suspect."

Disappointed, Lillian returns home and goes to her computer. Perhaps the police will never need her testimony, but for her own satisfaction, she records every sensation that she can remember, along with the time and the date. Her memory generally stays clear about everything, but somehow she wants to record the facts on paper as well as in her brain.

The evening news on television also reports that the authorities have a suspect in custody.

The next day, Lillian phones the police and asks for the officer in charge of the murder at Mimi's Muffin Shop.

"Hello, I'm the lady who keeps trying to help you identify the murderer at Mimi's Muffin Shop."

The officer says he knows of her and her dog. "If you have a suspect, put him in a lineup, and I'll pick him out for you."

"How's that, ma'am?" came the policeman's voice on the other end of the line. "Are you trying to tell me you want to walk down the lineup and smell each person? I don't think we could do that. Witnesses view the lineup from behind a one-way window where they can't be seen. Often we use felons already in detention for the lineup. These fellows would see you. They might hate you for helping us. You'd be really vulnerable after that, and besides…Well, thanks anyway for the call."

Annoyed, Lillian replaces the receiver. *He didn't finish his sentence.* She can tell that, because of her blindness, the officer doesn't believe she could help. *Why can no one understand?*

A week later, Lillian has Harold drop her and Pickwick off at the courthouse where the murderer is to be arraigned. Someone shows her to a room that smells of lemon oil on varnished wood. An attendant walks her down the centre aisle of the courtroom and tells her that a pew on her left has some vacancies. She moves down the bench until she senses nearness to another person and sits. Pickwick settles himself underneath the bench behind her feet. Before the start of the proceedings, another person slides in at the end of her bench.

The only words spoken by the accused are subdued. "Not guilty, Your Honour." Lillian finds it hard to compare his voice with that of the man who shouted at her as he came down the hallway. She listens to the judge and the lawyers. Their comments fit the crime as she knows it. Lillian realizes that the police seem to have managed without her.

Near the end of proceedings another spectator pushes in at the end of the pew. The man sitting next to Lillian crowds closer.

"Excuse me," he says with a gravelly voice to Lillian as they crush together on the bench. Lillian hears Pickwick quietly sniffing at the man's footwear. *That's odd,* she thinks, *Pickwick never sniffs at people when he's in harness.* She wonders if the man's feet have crowded the dog's space.

Then, for some unknown reason, Lillian finds that her brain has shifted into overdrive. *That voice, its gruffness—what is it about him? The smoke in his clothes. The smell of his hair. There's something about his very essence—*

Why, it's him, the murderer, here, sitting beside me! That's why Pickwick's fussing. He remembers the smell of the man's boots.

Lillian's head continues to spin. *The police have the wrong man—but how can I tell them when they won't listen? How can I tell them without alerting the fellow beside me? What am I to do?*

For a moment Lillian thinks. *I know; I'll cause a scene.*

She rises up in her seat, wailing, "Let me out of here! There's no oxygen! I'm going to faint. I can't see. Where's the door?"

She drags herself in front of the startled people sitting in her pew and struggles to gain the centre aisle. They draw back and let her pass. On purpose she paws her way from pew to pew down the aisle towards the judge, making the biggest commotion she can muster.

"No, no, I came in at the back of the room," she yells as if talking to herself. "I need to go the other direction to find the door." And she turns and grasps her way through the spectators who crowd the aisle as she makes her way towards the door, until she feels the grasp of a hand that's determined to assist her. Undetected, Pickwick, fearing for his mistress, crawls under the benches to the back of the room and reaches her just inside the door. Lillian feels his snout rub her leg and grabs the harness.

The judge pounds his gavel.

"Please be seated, everyone. Take your seats while this is resolved. We'll resume in a few minutes." The judge then goes to his chambers.

The hand that grabbed her releases its grip but remains a presence at her elbow. The person says, "I'm the courtroom attendant. This way, ma'am."

Lillian clutches at the hand upon her sleeve and draws the man into the hallway. "Quick," she says. "Take me to the judge."

Astounded by her sudden change of demeanour, the court attendant does as she asks. When he knocks softly on the judge's door, Lillian grabs for the door handle and bursts into the judge's chambers.

"Judge, you must listen to me. The police have the wrong man. I may be blind, but I witnessed the murderer leaving the crime, and so did my dog. I know what I smelled and heard. I'm sure I can finger the murderer. He's in the spectator's gallery right now, sitting on the bench where I was sitting. The man in custody is telling the truth when he says he didn't do it. If you can't trust my judgment, believe in Pickwick, my dog. He's very smart."

"Are you talking about the man who sat on your right?" asks the judge. Lillian agrees. The judge had noticed the fellow for his intense observation of the proceedings. Lillian suspects that the judge is smiling when he adds, "This should be interesting."

From the tone of his voice, Lillian wants to shake the man for being amused by her offer. *He's listening as if this is a game,* she thinks, *but at least he's listening.*

To prevent spectators from leaving early, the judge asks the attendant to return to the courtroom and assure everyone that the proceedings will continue immediately. Then he leads Lillian and Pickwick through a door off his chambers. Lillian presses her ear against the door and hears the judge call in the lawyers. He explains what he intends to do. She hears them leave the room. After a few minutes the judge returns to her.

"We asked some of the spectators to help us with a 'pending case' until we reconvene," the judge tells her. "No one objected. I suppose they were curious about helping. Then we picked out the man you suggested and four others who look quite dissimilar so they won't suspect our motive. These men are assembled in a nearby interrogation room. I thought a loose circle rather than a lineup might make them feel more at ease. We've given each of them a number. You won't have Pickwick, so I'll walk with you. We'll pass in front of each man, and he'll shout out his number as we approach. From the location of the voice, please try to direct your face at each fellow as if you can see, so you don't alert any of them that you are blind. After we leave the room, tell me the number of the man you think is the murderer."

Lillian and the judge walk around the circle of men. Lillian listens to the voice as each number is shouted. She passes close enough to sniff the essence of each man. When she has left the room, Lillian says she is quite sure it is number four.

"Now we'll let Pickwick have his turn. Say nothing to the dog by voice or through hand movements on the harness. After I start you in the right direction, just lead him past the men. We'll watch to see if Pickwick reacts to anyone."

Pickwick enters with Lillian. He passes by number one and number two in his usual sedate fashion. Pickwick ignores number three and moves right on to number four, with eyes intent on the man's face. The dog's hackles rise. A low growl starts deep in his throat. He plants his front paws at the man's feet and tenses his haunches, then throws back his head and lets out a vicious growl, like a tiger cornering his prey.

Vibrations through the handle of the harness and Pickwick's menacing growl make Lillian's knees tremble. Every instinct in her screams, "Danger! Run for your life!" yet training forces her to abide by the security offered by her dog. She grasps his harness handle tighter.

Lillian hears the man suck in his breath. She senses that he's recognized her and knows he's been trapped.

"You!" shouts his malevolent voice. "If it weren't for that damn dog, I would'a bashed in your brains when I had the chance." To mark his words he raises a fist and thumps it towards Lillian. Pickwick's harness is quick to force her back a few paces. She hears a moment of scuffling, then, in a speck of silence, the click of handcuffs.

⁓

Minutes later the judge reconvenes those in the courtroom. "New evidence has come to light. We have just found two witnesses to the crime. The case against the defendant is dismissed."

When the courtroom clears, the judge congratulates Lillian. "The room where we had the lineup is equipped with camera surveillance. You won't have to appear at his trial. The film will show that he convicted himself. And may I add, you and Pickwick make quite a team. Your ability to sense things is amazing. Thanks to the two of you, justice has been served."

POTTERING AROUND

II

Just off the master bedroom at the front of the house, Lillian sits on her second-floor balcony, enjoying the warmth of the morning sun and the sound of birds cheeping in the trees that grow in her garden. With stubby fingers, she pushes greying hair away from her ears and listens to the serenity of her surroundings, then lowers her hand to pat her black lab guide dog, Pickwick.

She speaks to Pickwick. She often speaks to Pickwick, for he is her constant friend and companion.

"Boring, isn't it, Pickwick. No vehicles passing to guess their make, no people on the sidewalk chattering about problems—not even birds fighting over their pecking order. At least yesterday we could imagine the new neighbour mowing his lawn with the roar of his machine shattering the stillness. What we need is a little excitement—something to do on these long summer days."

Pickwick stretches and flops on his side to continue his silent vigil, even though he is not in harness.

Lillian knows her boredom will soon end, for Emily, her long-time friend from across the street, comes every Tuesday morning for a visit. They'll chat and enjoy the iced tea that Lillian prepared earlier and poured into a thermos jug, which now sits waiting for them on the balcony table. There are two lawn chairs on the balcony, complete with padded blue-and-yellow flowered cushions.

A voice from next door blasts Lillian's ears. "Jake! When are you gonna cut the damn grass?"

That must be the wife of the new neighbour, thinks Lillian. *What's her problem? He mowed the lawn yesterday.* Lillian adds the name "Jake" to her vast memory bank.

"Yeah, yeah, pussycat, in a moment," shouts Jake. Lillian hears the opening of a vehicle door. It must be parked in the laneway that separates their two homes. She hears the click of lady's high heels on asphalt. Lillian usually greets Emily at the front door, but today is different; she wants to listen for more of the neighbour's sharp words.

Emily lets herself in and comes up to the second-floor balcony off the master bedroom. Pickwick rises and stands in front of the sliding door to determine if he approves of the ascending footsteps and the approach of the slender lady with platinum-dyed hair.

As Emily steps onto the deck, Lillian raises her finger to her lips. "Shhh. I'm eavesdropping on the neighbours." Lillian uses the hand motion and this simple, direct sentence because Emily is deaf. Lillian turns her head so Emily can read the words she whispers. Her face glows with excitement. "I think they're about to have a fight! You watch, and I'll listen. She wants him to cut the grass, and I heard their mower yesterday."

Emily creeps to the end of the decking to spy on the new neighbours. The lady is on her front porch talking adamantly to Jake, judging from the waving of her arms. Emily can't hear the conversation but catches some of it by reading their lips. Jake mouths the word "Mugs" when addressing the woman.

"Grass, Lillian? Did you say 'Cut the grass'? They aren't talking about the lawn. Her lips seemed to form the word 'marijuana.' They must be talking about pot. Do you think they are growing marijuana in their basement?"

Lillian grins. "If they are, Emily, we could have great fun investigating them. What danger could two over-the-hill housewives be to them? Why, with one of us blind and the other deaf, they won't even suspect we're entertaining ourselves with a little detective work. It's not as if we'd turn them in to the police. They'll know I'm blind because of Pickwick, and they won't realize you can read lips or speak if you don't let on. Come, have some iced tea and tell me what you saw down there."

Emily is delighted with the prospect of spying on the new neighbours to fill her soundless days. Lillian can make life so much fun. Emily reports that the vehicle is a rusted old black delivery van and that Jake has planted a wonderful assortment of flowers in the garden encircling his house. From her comments, Lillian knows she will always think of Jake as having messy brown hair, while the woman will have straight black hair and no makeup. They'll be in blue jeans and T-shirts. Emily thinks that both are in their mid-thirties.

Lillian pours the iced tea with her index finger hooked over the rim of the glass to judge when to stop pouring. Next she turns on her audio recorder, and they begin compiling notes and planning a strategy for their sleuthing. Lillian lifts the cordless phone from the table and dials her son, even though she knows he's at work. She leaves a message for him to search the Internet for information on growing marijuana and asks that he return her call in the evening, then adds, "No, I'm not going to start smoking pot, silly boy."

Crash, crackle, crackle! After the crash, Lillian hears a string of swear words.

"Someone has dropped something in the lane. Quick, Emily, look and see what's happening."

Emily dashes to the corner of the balcony and peeks over the railing in her best detective pose. Jake has dropped the top half of a stack of green plastic flowerpots at the back of his delivery van. They try to decide if the flowerpots are for growing marijuana or if they have something to do with all the bedding plants Jake has planted around his house.

"Now he's picking up the pieces of the few that broke," whispers Emily, "and sweeping the asphalt with a garden broom to remove any little pieces of plastic—as if anyone would care." The event goes onto Lillian's audio recorder. They determine that their sleuthing operation will be more successful if the neighbours don't see them together. They will compare notes each evening after dark when it is safe to cross the street unnoticed. The neighbours go inside, and Emily returns home.

⌒∞⌒

Late that evening, with Pickwick, Lillian rushes over to her friend's house.

"My son phoned. He thinks the two of us are completely mad, but he knows he can't stop us from having our fun. He says we must check for covered-over basement windows, a sound much like a clothes-dryer exhaust going all the time, the particular odour of marijuana, either in the neighbour's house or coming from the exhaust vent, and a possible lack of friendliness. He also mentioned watching for pipes needed for their ventilation system and said we should keep an eye on the van's schedule, *and* he said to be careful if we insist on being so nosy. They might be dangerous." The women are delighted with his information and reproach. Immediately, they put their imaginations into high gear to determine the detective work they will have to undertake.

The next morning, Lillian waits until she hears someone across the lane come outside. She directs Pickwick to lead her down the driveway, then left towards the side lane. Purposefully, she walks on the right-hand side of the lane with the hope of bumping into the neighbour's van. Dutiful Pickwick tries to lead her around the vehicle, but she ignores the dog until she bumps her shin and yells a convincing "Ow" to catch the neighbour's attention.

"Are you okay, lady?" It's Jake's voice. As if holding her forehead, she listens for the faint voice of her watch—*10 a.m., and he's not at work,* she notes.

"Yes. I haven't had my dog very long, and sometimes he doesn't give me the right signals."

If Pickwick knew what I just said about him, thinks Lillian, *he'd be disgusted with my lie. It's a good thing he doesn't understand everything I say.* Having caught the man's attention, Lillian starts the conversation she has planned, and Pickwick sits.

"My husband tells me you have ringed the house with beautiful bedding plants. When did you move in?"

His answer is curt. "Why do you want to know?"

Lillian takes a deep breath and searches for a fast answer. "I suppose because I'm your neighbour. I'm trying to be friendly. Are you renting?" she asks, defying the odds that the man will divulge anything.

"Renting. Sorry, lady, but the missus expects me back in the house. I just came out to get something for her."

Lillian walks on down the side lane. Behind her she hears a noise that sounds like tin bumping on tin as the man climbs the steps of his back porch.

She continues her walk along the back lane in case Jake is watching. Pickwick enjoys watering the weeds in the lane, and they return home.

Lillian reports to her friend: 10 a.m., renting, clanking tin that might be pipes for ductwork, and her need for a fast reply when she was taken aback by Jake's coldness. They wonder what marijuana smells like and plan on devising some way of determining this. They certainly can't ask friends. Their friends wouldn't know, and the grapevine would have the two of them smoking pot in no time. They put the problem aside for another day and plan Emily's strategy.

❧

Dressed in a deep-rose slacks suit, with a measuring cup in hand and a short note, Emily knocks on Jake's front door. An expressionless Mugs opens the door. Emily smiles and passes Mugs the note and the cup. It reads, "I'm deaf. Partway through baking a cake I found I'm short half a cup of flour. I saw you move in at the end of winter and thought that this would be a good opportunity to meet you folks. My name is Emily."

Mugs nods, leaves Emily standing on the front doorstep, and turns towards the back of the house without introducing herself. Immediately, Emily steps into the front hall of the house, as if invited, in order to have a look around and sniff the air.

As Mugs returns down the hall, she scowls at Emily's presumption to step inside. Her lips are moving as if talking to someone in the kitchen. "The bag from across the street came into the house."

Emily has trouble keeping from laughing. She decides she must be very sweet, mouth "Thank you," and leave before her facial expression gives away her understanding of Mugs' comment.

That evening, Emily reports humidity in the house, an odd sweet fragrance that she likened to very pungent flowers, nice furniture, and details of the less than friendly welcome. While they continue with their detective plans, they wonder why the house, furniture, and garden are nice but their vehicle is a wreck, and the words spoken by Jake and Mugs don't fit with the conversation of other neighbours.

Emily sets a mug of coffee on the breakfast-nook table in front of Lillian, then sits across from her with a mug for herself. They continue to talk.

"I've decided that I'll ask the canine squad to teach Pickwick what marijuana smells like," says Lillian. "If they ask me why I want the dog to recognize the smell of marijuana, I'll say that my son brings his school friends home, and I want to know if any of them smoke pot. I'm sure Pickwick will learn the smell very quickly."

"But you don't have a son still living at home," says Emily.

"Does that matter?" asks Lillian with a laugh. "They won't check."

The following morning, Lillian phones the canine squad. The officer explains that police-trained dogs are very aggressive. It would be impossible for Pickwick to join one of their dog-training exercises. He also tells her, "You are right about one thing—you need a dog's keen sense of smell to recognize green marijuana plants still under cultivation. The plants have such a mild odour that only a trained dog would be able to detect it. Drying the leaves or smoking marijuana is different. That's a smell anyone can recognize. It's sort of a sweet, pungent odour, much like that of a passing skunk."

Lillian goes to her audio recorder and makes notes about the two odours and ductwork for Emily. During the day, Emily has purchased a small notebook like detectives use on TV and recorded all of their findings to date. They entitle the notebook "Record of Culpability."

"Oh my, Pickwick, isn't this fun? If only I could teach you the smell of marijuana."

Frustrated, Lillian decides to phone the drug squad. Only yesterday, she heard on TV about a big drug bust with hundreds of plants confiscated. Then she has a new idea, bold and much more likely to get fast results. Either good or bad, she knows it will be exciting.

The women get together again that evening. "Emily, drive Pickwick and me down to the central police station tomorrow. It's amazing how people stand back when a blind person and dog strut with determination. I'm going to walk right in and ask for the drug squad. I'll say to them, 'What harm will it do to let Pickwick smell the green marijuana you have locked up in the evidence room?' Why, I might even get some soft-hearted policeman to give me a leaf or two." Then she chuckles. "If I pull it off, we can smoke it in celebration.

I'll try to get Pickwick to put his foot in the marijuana, and he can relive the smell until he gets it licked off."

❦

The next morning, in keeping with undercover detective work, Lillian and Pickwick walk east down the street. When they round the corner and are out of sight a block away, Emily is waiting for them in her handsome old silver Cadillac, and they drive to the police station. Emily takes Lillian to the entrance of the station and points her in the right direction, then waits.

Lillian knows people will be flabbergasted when they see the steady strut and swishing blue skirt of a grey-haired lady with a guide dog. She hears them stepping out of the way to let her pass. When Pickwick stops, Lillian figures that they have arrived at some sort of destination.

"Officer, please direct us to the drug squad," she announces to the whole room. The room melts into silence. "I must see an officer there at once!"

Lillian has no idea what the desk sergeant thinks of her officious demand. She decides that he has no ideas about her either, for miraculously, instead of asking questions, he calls for a young-sounding officer to direct her to the drug unit. She laughs to herself—*I bet that sergeant decided he'd rather the drug squad figure me out than have my loud voice embarrass him in front of that room full of people.*

When they arrive at the drug unit, the junior policeman leaves them. Lillian completely changes her demeanour and quietly spills out her wish to let Pickwick smell the marijuana they have in the evidence room. She explains that she has some new weeds in her garden and thinks they might be marijuana. She is sure Pickwick could recognize it by smell easier than she could detect marijuana plants by touch.

"Why that's preposterous! I can't let your dog trail around in the evidence room," says the man in front of her.

Lillian does not want to fail when she's this close to getting her way. She listens for the sound of other officers in the room. The man is alone, as far as she can tell, so she tries a new strategy.

"You're all alone," she gushes sweetly. "Who would know the difference if you let my dog smell the marijuana? You'd make a blind lady very happy."

Lillian has no idea what changes take place in the man's facial expression. Will he say "Clap her in irons" for trying to bribe him? She waits.

He clears his throat and speaks in a low voice. "Okay, I just happen to be marking one of the bags of evidence. Come on, quickly now, bring your dog around here and let him have his sniff." Then he takes her arm and directs her around the desk.

When he stops, she takes one more step, with the hope of kicking the bag and spilling it. She doesn't succeed, but when the man sees her lurch and jumps to her assistance, he spills it himself. Lillian pushes on Pickwick's harness to urge her dog forward. From the officer's protests she is sure that Pickwick is standing on the marijuana while he is trying to clean up the mess. Just as the officer asks for her name and address, they hear footsteps in the hall.

"That's my supervisor coming," says the drug squad officer. His voice sounds nervous. "Go! Get out of here." Without giving her name, she smiles and tips her head sideways this way and that, as if trying to find the words to say thank you, and leaves.

She knows she must turn left from the office, but what next, with nobody to guide her? She feels lost. *Maybe Pickwick knows how to get out of here,* she thinks. She says, "Pickwick, straight, straight to the outside door," and Pickwick leads off. At the first intersecting hallway she hears the doors of lockers being slammed and urges Pickwick to go straight ahead.

Pickwick continues on a few paces, then stops. Lillian finds herself in a closet that smells of cleaning equipment. *The closet door is open!* Exasperated, she feels the moulding of the doorway. *A "T" intersection,* she gasps to herself. *I didn't realize we passed one coming in.* Lillian suspects that Pickwick wants out of this strange place as badly as she does.

She finds the turn in the corridor, and the next thing she knows, after two more turns, Emily is taking her arm. In the car they wonder if Pickwick learned anything about marijuana. Certainly, he's licking his paws.

◇◈◇

On Saturday, Lillian and Pickwick walk once again down the side lane towards the back of the lot. Lillian does her best to listen for an exhaust fan and sniff for an odd odour, but she hears nothing and can smell only the fragrant flowers planted around the neighbour's house. As the van is not parked in the lane and she hears nobody in their yard, Lillian successfully manages to knock over their garbage pail along the back fence. Jake rushes from the house onto his back porch.

"What are you doing with my garbage can, lady?"

Lillian puts on her stupid-blind-person act and fumbles to right the metal container and make the lid flop off. Hidden by the boards in the fence, she quickly runs her hand into the can to see if she can find any chips of plastic from the broken flowerpots. There is no garbage in the can, but she finds something at the bottom that feels about right for plastic. She pockets her finding with sheer exhilaration. Lillian slips the lid onto the uprighted garbage can, smiles like an angel, and turns to continue down the lane.

Pickwick rather likes the new territory but stands alert until Lillian removes his harness and attaches his leash to give him permission to relieve himself. When the dog has personalized every fencepost along the back lane, they return home.

Lillian puts the card in her living room window that signals Emily to go to the nearby Tim Horton's for a clandestine meeting. Lillian wants her to examine the "piece of evidence." Like a real detective, she slips it into a small plastic bag.

At the coffee shop, Emily turns the new evidence over in her fingers. It is indeed a slightly curved piece of green plastic. They decide to have Pickwick sniff it later that evening when he won't be distracted by all the restaurant patrons.

∽∞∾

Pickwick shows no interest in the piece of plastic. They feel he learned nothing at the police station. Their investigation is going nowhere.

"Why is it," says Emily, "that marijuana should have a certain odour, but we can't find a trace of it?"

"Never mind if we're investigating something that doesn't exist, Emily. It seems great fun. I say we dream up more plans."

Over the next few days, Lillian continues her walks to the back lane with Pickwick to have the opportunity for a friendly "Hello" if the neighbours are outside in the yard. Bit by bit, she feels sure the neighbours are warming to her. With binoculars, Emily determines the make of the black delivery van and notes the license plate. She takes walks in various directions until she has determined that all of the basement windows are covered over in black. Jake often watches her but says nothing. She wonders if he suspects she is snooping, for he comes into the yard every time she goes walking. Emily adds a few ordinary trips to put him off. Both women keep track of the van. Lillian records what she hears from her balcony, and Emily watches until late in the evening from a darkened upstairs window. All information goes into their notebook.

❦

After a week of walking Pickwick to the back lane, Lillian senses that Mugs is alone, sweeping the back porch. Lillian knows folks are often curious about a blind person's lack of sight, so, after her friendly "Hello" she works her way over to the side gate of Mugs' fence near the corner of the house and starts in on a good yarn.

"I could see when I was a child. Why, I could jump the lines in hopscotch, skip rope, bat a baseball, and play just about any game. In my teens I learned to drive our boat. Now I can't even walk down a dock without Pickwick or a person to guide me. I started to lose my sight when I was twenty, so I have the luxury of knowing the different colours. In my own way, I still remember the blue of the sky, the greens of bushes and trees, and the wonderful riot of colours in my father's flower garden."

Mugs listens with only the occasional, "Oh, my," or "Really!" They move to the back porch steps to sit while Lillian continues her story.

"The retinas of my eyes started to split. They mended them with laser treatments, but after a while the doctors couldn't do any more. Now, if you lead me around your home and name the different flowers your husband planted, I'll tell you the colour just to show you how well I remember."

Challenged, Mugs falls for the bait Lillian has set to give her the opportunity to circle the house with the hope of hearing an exhaust fan. Mugs leads Lillian and Pickwick past the flowers across the back of the house. Lillian amazes Mugs with her wonderful memory of flowers' colours.

They turn along the far side of the house. That's when Lillian first hears the soft throb of an exhaust fan. She sniffs for an odour—any odour, even laundry detergent—but smells nothing but the flowers. Pickwick promptly sits. She urges him on. He takes two steps and sits again. Lillian wonders if her dog is trying to tell her something.

Mugs calls from the front corner of the house when she sees they have dropped behind. From the sound of her voice, she is annoyed. "Why have you stopped? We've only gone halfway around the house. Why is Pickwick sitting?"

Lillian realizes that her dog has detected the smell of marijuana. Would Mugs suspect them for stopping right at the vent? She feels a cold sweat break out on her forehead.

"The short heels of my shoes caught in the grass. I nearly fell," Lillian replies. "Pickwick's waiting for me to get my balance again," and she drags him away from the vent, which must be hidden by the flowers.

Walking past the garden at the front of the house, Lillian starts to cut short her story about blindness. She can't wait to rush home and put the card in her living room window so Emily will meet her at Tim Horton's. She must tell her about hearing the fan.

❦

At Tim Horton's, Emily starts talking as soon as she sees her friend.

"Lillian, we missed something! I said Mugs' house had a sweet fragrant odour when I borrowed the flour, almost like strong pungent flowers. Your notes from the canine squad officer stated that marijuana smells skunky when smoked. I bet she and Jake were smoking pot in the kitchen and that was the cause of the smell. No wonder she was angry with me for coming into the house. She thought I would recognize the smell. It's a good thing I was too naive to know the difference between smelly flowers and pot. It helped me to keep a straight face."

The ladies take their hot chocolate and box of donut holes to a table in the corner of the coffee shop. Lillian tells of Pickwick's reaction when she circled the neighbour's house admiring the flowers and found the vent.

Emily seems disappointed with the story. "We've found the fan, the windows are darkened, and Pickwick smelled the marijuana. That means we've finished our detective work. Everything points to them growing marijuana in the basement. We only checked up on them for a little self-entertainment. It's been great fun, but now we have nothing more to investigate."

"I know one thing, Emily."

"What's the point, Lillian? The police won't be interested in a little home-grow operation claimed by a blind woman and her deaf friend. Like your son, they'll think we're out of our minds. They want to catch the big operators."

The women sit quietly munching on donut holes. Lillian takes a Milk-Bone from her purse and gives Pickwick his treat.

"We haven't followed through on the van schedule, Emily. We could do that. Perhaps Jake sells the stuff or dries it at some other location. We could check for an exhaust fan there and try for a whiff of the skunky marijuana odour. Let's finish our investigating."

"The van? Oh yes, lets check on the van!" says Emily.

Delighted with the new idea, they take the box of remaining donut holes and hurry home. No one is outside at Jake's house. Together, they rush up Emily's front steps. In the living room they pore over their notes. Jake seems to leave home about 11 p.m. quite often. Emily moves her Cadillac onto the front street. She adjusts the special mirror that her late husband installed so she could read the lips of her passenger when driving.

At 10 p.m., with the shadows of summer nightfall upon them, the two ladies climb into the car and slouch down low. They are in luck; Jake leaves home at 11. The women duck even lower in their seats and hold their breath, as if that will help them appear to be invisible. He drives past them. The residential streets have no traffic. Emily's old-model car allows her to tail him some distance without headlights. When he turns a corner she switches on her lights and follows around after him. After four intersections, he turns right and parks halfway down the block. Emily pulls to the curb three houses back.

She walks past the house Jake has entered. He puts on the light in the front hall but no other light. Emily checks the address and hurries back to her car, afraid that he'll come out of the house and recognize her.

"Lillian," she puffs, "he didn't seem to need a light in any of the rooms. I think he went into the basement, yet the windows showed no light."

"He must have another grow operation in there, Emily."
They write the address on a fresh page of the notebook.

After ten minutes, Jake returns to his van and drives a
few blocks to another house. Again, Emily checks the address,
and soon Jake leads them to a third house to repeat the pro-
cess again. At this house, within minutes, Jake leaves, carrying
a large bundle out to the van.

Surprised by his quick return and hardly away from the
house where Jake stopped, Emily turns her back and holds
her hands wide while thrust in in her pockets to look like
a fat person under the streetlights. She can hardly keep herself from racing to the protection of her car. She's sure Jake
stopped to look at her before driving off.

"Where do you think he's going now, Lillian? He seems
to be heading out of our district and driving towards the
southeast."

They follow in and out through traffic for ten minutes.
The storefronts begin to look less prosperous, then seedy.
There are drunks and garbage cans on the street. "This isn't a
very nice part of town, Lillian. Maybe we are foolish to keep
following him."

"Don't be chicken, Emily. What can happen to us? The
car doors are locked, and I have my cellphone and a dog with
a good growl."

Emily reduces the distance between the van and her car,
for the side streets are coming more often, and she doesn't
want to lose him.

"Lillian! There's a police car behind me flashing his lights.
I'll have to stop." Emily winds down her window as the officer
approaches. He stoops and pokes his head in to look around.
In that position Emily easily reads his lips.

"What are you doing in this district lady? A fine Cadillac following a broken down black van. I picked you up some blocks back, and it seems you are either up to no good or about to get yourself in trouble."

Emily can still see the taillights of the black van. "Please, officer," she cries, "don't stop us. We're following that van because we know he grows marijuana in his basement and at three other houses. We're trying to see where he's going."

"It's just as well I stopped you. I'll take over following him, and you nice ladies go on home. This is police work. You know, ladies, there's easier ways to get yourself a secret supply of pot." By now, Emily cannot see his lips, but Lillian hears his facetious remark and is annoyed.

With red and blue lights flashing and siren whining, the police car whizzes past the Cadillac and closes the distance on the van.

"Emily, that officer was laughing at us. I could hear it in his voice—laughing at the idea that two women our age were following a marijuana grower. He's likely chasing Jake to amuse us. Going home is no fun." Lillian smiles. "I say we follow the police car to see what happens."

Emily grins and follows along in the chase.

"We seem to be going faster, Lillian. Jake must have spotted the police car. I think he's trying to get away." Emily increases her speed.

One corner follows after another. Tires screech and Lillian whoops with pleasure as her body flops a bit this way and that in the shoulder harness. After flying sideways on the first fast corner, Pickwick braces himself on the floor between the front and back seats.

Emily looks ahead and sees two white cars come from a dark side street into the space between her car and the police car. As the two vehicles turn, under the glow of streetlights, Emily reads the word "POLICE" in blue lettering. Immediately, she sees their red and blue lights begin to flash. Sirens wail. As if without thought, Emily finds herself pursuing the three police cars at high speed.

Emily's car squeals around the next corner, then begins to slow down. "This is lunacy, Lillian. I'm going to turn off. I'm likely to crash the car and get us both killed." Lillian gives in, and Emily turns into the next street, only to find it is a narrow back lane.

"I have no idea where we are in town, Lillian. I think I should make a U-turn and go back onto that main road we just left so we don't get lost." Emily starts the turn.

Lillian continues to listen to the scream of the sirens. They fade—seem to change direction—then become more distinct again.

Lillian slaps at Emily's knee to gain her attention. "What's happening, Emily? The sirens are getting louder!"

Emily is too busy trying to turn the car around to lip-read what Lillian is saying about the sirens. Her old Cadillac is too long to make the turn easily. She cranks the steering wheel this way and that as she drives forward and backwards in the narrow lane, determined not to dent the chrome.

Halfway through the U-turn, the car headlights shine squarely upon a red brick building. She backs up in the little space she has and again yanks on the steering wheel. The sirens grow louder.

Headlights flash around the corner at the other end of the lane. A vehicle bears down on them at high speed. Lillian says that the motor sounds like a van.

Emily darts her eyes towards the oncoming vehicle, then screams, "He's going to hit us broadside." She squeezes her eyes shut, expecting the speeding vehicle to crash into her late husband's pride and joy. Three police cars, with lights flashing and sirens screaming, follow into the lane in persistent pursuit. The van can't pass the Cadillac with Emily straight across the lane still trying to manoeuvre her long car through the end of the U-turn.

Brakes squeal on pavement. There's a smell of burning rubber. Emily sees the van stop within inches. It tries to reverse direction. The squad cars block its escape. Emily stops trying to drive her car in order to keep Lillian happy with a constant dialogue of what is happening.

"The police have their guns pulled. Four officers are sneaking up on the van, two on each side. They've yanked the doors open. The driver is getting out with his hands up. What if it's Jake? The man is the same size and weight. Here come the handcuffs. The other policemen are searching the back of the van. They've found that bundle. Now they're walking him to a police car with an officer on each side, hanging on to him by the elbows. The dome light is on. Yes. It is Jake!"

"Imagine, Lillian, our detective work has actually caught a criminal! Haven't we done well!"

Lillian hears footsteps walking towards her side of the car. She lowers the window. It's a policeman. The women turn his way, smile, and square their shoulders, ready to accept his compliments and thanks.

"You two!" barks the policeman. "I thought I told you to go home." Pickwick gives a loud growl at the policeman's unpleasant voice. The growl causes the officer to jump back from the open window. He seems at a loss for words when he sees that the dog is in harness.

Lillian directs her frosted glasses and face towards the sound of the officer's voice. "Officer, you'll have to face my friend, Emily, so she can read your lips when you speak," says Lillian calmly. "That's right. She's deaf and I'm blind, but we're not dumb. Here is the information we gathered while investigating our neighbour when we thought he was growing marijuana. You'll discover he has at least four home-grow operations. I imagine he was headed to this part of town because the air is polluted by industry. Foul air will hide his drying operation. You'll have to find that on your own." She smiles and hands the notebook with her personal address card slipped beneath its front cover to the officer. "If there is any information you need," she says sweetly, "just call on us. Good night."

The policeman stands speechless, wondering how this woman has stolen the moment from him. Emily completes the turn.

Totally satisfied with their sleuthing, the two drive off into the night while Pickwick determines that his growl was superb.

MEXICAN HOLIDAY

III

Lillian hears the wheels of the undercarriage locking into position...tires bumping on the tarmac...engines roaring in reverse. She knows they have arrived in Acapulco.

She speaks to her black lab guide dog as the plane taxies towards the airport building. "Come, Pickwick—into your harness." She jokes with the dog while deplaning with her husband, Harold. "Not every dog gets a winter vacation in Mexico for five years running."

Once on the ground Pickwick is ready to guide Lillian through the multitude of people. Warm, humid air blasts through Lillian's clothing and across her skin as they near the exit of the air-conditioned airport. She waits beside a potted palm near the doors while Harold retrieves their bags.

The crowds begin to thin. She hears footsteps approaching—not Harold's.

"Hola, Señora ['ola, say-nior-a]. You want taxi? I am good taxi driver. I have nice car. I take your dog. You drive with me, si?"

Before Lillian can reply, Harold arrives with the bags. They know from past experience that many Mexican people are uneasy when they see the big black dog. Locals don't recognize the guide-dog harness, and many refuse to allow Pickwick into their taxis. The couple nod to the driver, and gallantly he loads himself down with their luggage and leads the way to his taxi.

"I am José [Hoe zay]. I learn good Eengleesh, no? This my taxi. All mine," he adds with enthusiasm. "'Otel Paraiso, Paradise, si?"

They climb into the taxi and head for the hotel. Lillian sits gingerly with her hands in her lap, quite sure that she can smell the odour of the hundreds of perspiring passengers who have used the taxi before her.

"Nice cab, no?" José has started again. "See my flags?" José taps the top of his windshield. "One sticker for each country I drive. You look for flags on taxi, and you hire me. I be your taxi man, no?" Lillian wonders if the flags restrict his view.

"Have you a Canadian flag?" she asks to humour him.

"Mañana, Señora. I put new sticker for you. I be your taxi man *for sure,* si?"

The car travels at moderate speeds, moves gently around corners, and translates the rumble of wheels on asphalt and potholes alike. Lillian decides that José is indeed a good driver. She wonders how a man with such a young voice has managed to buy a cab of his own. He must have worked hard to learn English. As the cab winds its way along the streets, she feels sure that Harold will look for José's flags and hire him the next time they need a cab.

The taxi has no air-conditioning except wide-open windows. As they drive to the hotel, Lillian can hear raw trumpets blaring the winding tempo of Mexican music in the street bars, the sound of many feet on the sidewalks, and the swish of passing bicycles. She sits back and enjoys it all. Mexico always seems to be so alive.

⚚

At the hotel, while still on the street, Lillian hears soft Spanish waltzes being piped through the hotel intercom. As José leaves the lobby after depositing their bags, she tries out her meager Spanish.

"Gracias, José; hasta luego ['asta loo ay go]."

⚚

"I hear loud voices at the desk, Harold. They're nearly shouting. What's going on?"

"Wait here, and I'll find out." Harold works his way to the desk to register and returns. "It seems a customer is furious because something was stolen from his room yesterday. I've registered. Our room is this way."

It is the first time for Harold and Lillian to stay at this hotel. The advertisement in the tour book pictured the hotel with a photo taken from the air. The photo showed a single-storey building that formed a square around a private central garden. Centred in the garden, palm trees and flowers surrounded a swimming pool, blue as sapphire.

Down a hallway, the bellhop finds their room number, and they enter a cool, quiet room.

"Lead me around the room once, Harold, and I'll know my way." Harold and Lillian start with their backs to the room door. They move off to the right along the wall and around the room, with Pickwick at Lillian's side. Harold pats the two chairs and the bed to show their position. He gives a quick turn of the cold water tap and flushes the toilet.

"There's more, Lillian. We have a balcony. Just a minute; I have to lift a length of wood they are using as a lock for the sliding door. Funny, it has a little hole drilled across one end of it. I wonder how that happened." He pushes open the door, and they step out into the fragrance and heat of the garden. He pats the two patio chairs and explains that the balcony is only a metre off the ground. They retreat to the cool of the room.

After unpacking clothes and Pickwick's bed, Lillian listens to her watch, calculates the time zone difference, and decides it is time for dinner.

⚬⚭⚬

"José!" Harold shouts. "Aqui [ah key]!" Harold waves at the waiting cabs. The taxi with the flag decals cuts out of the line-up and draws to the curb. A delighted José jumps to their assistance. Harold names "Club Pacifico" as their destination.

"Un momento, señor. I must phone my dispatcher and tell him where I am going." With that José speaks on his cell-phone in Spanish too rapid for Lillian to translate. *Yesterday José said he owned the taxi all by himself, and today he has a dispatcher—pretty organized,* thinks Lillian.

⚬⚭⚬

After dinner at Club Pacifico, they find José waiting for them and are quite pleased to have such a thoughtful driver. Again, he speaks into his cellphone, and they leave for the hotel.

In their hotel room Lillian thinks she can smell perspiration—not Harold's. Pickwick sniffs his way to the balcony door.

"Did you replace the bar in the door after we were on the balcony, Harold?"

"Sure did. I pulled the drapes, too, so we wouldn't get the morning sun." Lillian strokes the centreline of the curtains. They seem to be touching. She joins Harold as they turn in for the night.

◦◦◦

In the morning, Harold opens the room door to the hall. "I'm going down to the lobby to send an email. It has to go out first thing. I'll find José and see if he will take us south to the sand beach."

"I'll be fine," says Lillian. As the door closes it blocks out a brassy voice engaged in an argument at the end of the hall. Lillian and Pickwick walk to the sliding doors. She lifts the wooden bar and steps onto the balcony. She hears the scraping of a shovel on soil.

"I hear someone gardening, but I can't see you because I'm blind. Are you the gardener?"

"Si, señora. I am Miguel [Mig ail], the hotel gardener. I plant rose bush. I work hard to make nice garden, but people go straight to pool. They don't walk around to see my flowers."

From the balcony, Lillian hears the lock on the room door click. Harold must be back. "I will come this afternoon to walk in your garden, Miguel. Hasta luego." *Until next time,* she says to herself. *I got that phrase right,* and she steps back into the room.

"Oh! Señora." A startled housekeeping maid is reaching to make the bed. "I did not see you out there. I thought de room was empty."

"Entra, señorita. Esta bien." Having exhausted her small vocabulary of Spanish, Lillian turns to English. "You speak English very well—ah—what is your name?"

"Rosalia, señora. I had to learn de Eengleesh to get de job. My family have no money and many childrens, so I need de job."

"Do you like working here?"

"Yes and no. I like de job, but my supervisor, Maria, is not nice." Rosalia pauses while she moves on to the bathroom. "She calls me a stupid girl from de country. She tells people I am a thief, but I'm not. I can't be. I need de job."

Harold arrives. Rosalia goes to the sliding door, closes it, and replaces the wooden bar. They all leave together, Rosalia to continue cleaning and Harold, Lillian, and Pickwick for the beach. José is waiting. He makes his cellphone call, and they drive south along the coast road, heading for a strip of white sand with blue Pacific water glinting on the horizon. *Poor Rosalia,* thinks Lillian as they drive along.

Once the taxi stops, she finds the sun warm, and the sound of the softly rolling waves soon invites her to have a swim. She removes Pickwick's harness and clips a soft leash to his collar. Next, she slips the looped handle of the leash over a belt she fastens at her waist. Pickwick gyrates with delight at the prospects of going swimming. While Harold relaxes with a book, Lillian walks towards the sound of the waves. They are cold at first but so refreshing. They go forward with the waves washing into their faces until Lillian is swimming in shoulder-depth water.

"Oh, Pickwick, if only you could speak. Isn't this glorious? Give me a little woof if you are having fun." Pickwick coughs with a snoutful of saltwater. Lillian laughs.

"That's not a woof. Let's go closer to shore." She turns her back on the waves, knowing that this will direct them to shore and shallower water, where Pickwick's feet can touch bottom. They splash water at each other for a few moments, then dry themselves, stretched out on the sand.

Seagulls squeal overhead and a soft breeze lifts across her body, but Lillian cannot relax. Again, she thinks of Rosalia and her nasty supervisor. Was the brassy voice she heard in the hallway earlier the maid's supervisor, Maria, lashing out at some poor employee? Perhaps at Rosalia?

Harold closes his book.

"If you and Pickwick are dry, it's time to go. José is waiting up at the road."

⁕

In the hotel lobby, Lillian senses abnormal activity. It's quiet, with people whispering. She hears a girl sobbing. Harold tells her it is Rosalia in handcuffs being led away by the police. A woman is calling after them for all the guests in the lobby to hear, saying, "Yes, Detective Paredes, you have caught the thief who has been disturbing our guests."

"Harold, that is the same brassy voice I heard before. Is she by any chance in a hotel uniform—perhaps the supervisor of the housekeeping staff? Her name tag should read 'Maria' if it is."

Harold moves forward in the crowd, takes a better look at the woman and her hotel badge, and then he reports to Lillian that she has guessed correctly.

"Rosalia is not the thief, Harold. I'm good at guessing character, and I'm sure from the little snatch of conversation I had with Rosalia that they have the wrong person. I wonder if that supervisor has a reason to put the blame on her newest employee."

❧

Lillian finds this thought going over and over in her mind during lunch. They return to their room for a siesta during the heat of the day, but Lillian cannot sleep. She continues to think of Rosalia until Harold awakens.

"Pickwick and I want to walk in the garden. I promised Miguel, the gardener, that I would this afternoon." Harold shows Lillian where to find the doors leading to the garden and leaves to go to the newspaper stand.

"Pickwick, straight," commands Lillian. The dog sets out along the pathway that leads around the garden. Lillian enjoys the fragrance of roses, carnations, and oleander as they walk together. *Miguel is right*, thinks Lillian, *no one is walking in the garden, unless perhaps one person is ahead on the path.* Pickwick detours around something in the way.

Lillian stubs her toe and puts out her hands. They strike what feels like a sharp, stiff wire that's bent at the end. *It's sticking up above handles*, she thinks—*handles of shovels and rakes.* "Miguel, are you just ahead working in the garden?"

"Si, señora. I did not hear you coming."

A telephone starts to ring. The ring is very close.

"'Ello." Miguel shouts. *He must have a cellphone*, thinks Lillian. *The Mexican people are catching on to all of our electronic gadgets.* "Mas tardy [tarday]. Estoy trabajando [trabahan-do]," he says abruptly. This Lillian understands—"Later; I'm

40

working." It occurs to Lillian that had she not been there, he might have talked to the caller.

"Lo siento, for de call on mi telefono, señora. 'otel business." Miguel changes the subject. "You are nice. I put two pots of geraniums on your balcony. They are red."

Lillian says "Gracias" even though she is more concerned with tripping over them than knowing their colour, a colour that she cannot see. She continues her walk. As she passes by Miguel kneeling at the edge of the path, Pickwick growls softly. This scares the poor man into dropping the trowel from his hand. Pickwick then walks stoically straight ahead, again attending to his mistress's needs. She hurries the dog away, quite confused by Pickwick's unusual action.

When the heat and humidity seem too great in the garden, Lillian returns to the hotel lobby. She listens to her watch—five thirty. Pickwick knows which hallway to take and leads her towards their room.

Someone is talking behind a closed door along the hall. Lillian recognizes Maria's brassy voice. She speaks in angry tones, waits a few seconds, then speaks again—she is talking on a cellphone.

The talking ceases, the closed door opens, and Maria comes towards Lillian with solid, heavy footsteps, approaching quickly. Lillian flattens herself against the wall, and the stomping heels pass with little regard for her or Pickwick in the narrow passageway. Lillian's sharp hearing hears Maria muttering, "Perro del demonio [perrro del day-moan-ay-o]." Lillian translates the words to mean "damn dog" and wonders what the housekeeping supervisor has against her guide dog. *Certainly, the woman seems no nicer to hotel guests than she is on her cellphone,* thinks Lillian.

Again they ask José to drive them to dinner, this time to Fisherman's Wharf, and again he says he must call his dispatcher—she will want to know where he is going. He then drives on with a continuous stream of chatter until they come to the wharf with its loud pop music, Mexican style.

Lillian rubs the back of her neck against her collar as if to calm the little nerves that are rising to prickle her. Over a pina colado before dinner, thoughts fling themselves into her conversation with Harold. She pauses to allow these ideas to become cohesive, then starts to talk.

"I think I know who the thief is, and it's not Rosalia. Humour me, Harold. I have a plan. This evening we must walk in the hotel garden, and tomorrow morning you must take me to an expensive jewellery store. If the thief doesn't arrive in our room by noon tomorrow, nothing will happen, and I'll know I'm wrong."

Harold has seen his wife in this mood before and knows he cannot change her mind. He muses to himself that if Lillian finds the real thief by her detective work, it will likely be the highlight of her Mexican holiday, and so he agrees.

Back at the hotel, even though it is late in the evening, they enter the garden.

"Tell me, Harold, how many balconies have potted red geraniums on them?"

Harold looks around at all of the balconies, highlighted from shadow in the floodlights of the garden.

"Only one. Ours."

"Just as I thought."

They return to their room. Harold reads and Lillian sits, apparently thinking.

∽◯∽

In the morning, Lillian phones the police station and asks for Detective Paredes.

"I am a guest at the Hotel Paraiso, room 132. I've met the maid Rosalia, and I am sure she is not the thief. Please have a plainclothes policeman in the hotel garden this morning from 11 a.m. until 12:30, after lunch. He must watch the balcony with the potted red geraniums. I think he will see someone enter the room through the sliding doors. Also, please have an officer meet my husband, Harold, at the mayor's official residence at 12 noon."

Detective Paredes agrees to the plan because, as he says, he doesn't have a strong case against Rosalia, just the supervisor's word. Lillian hangs up the phone and chuckles.

"Harold, I think that detective is more interested in the outrageous idea of taking orders from a female hotel guest than he is in what might happen in the garden or at the mayor's mansion. I could sense the amusement in his voice."

Harold laughs. "Obviously, your exploits in Canada haven't reached the Mexican police yet. I'll be back for you in fifteen minutes. I want to see if my email has been answered."

Lillian finishes combing her thick greying hair. She is about to brush her teeth when the lock clicks. It is too soon for Harold's return. She wonders who will come to clean the room with Rosalia in jail.

"Housekeeping." It's the brassy voice of the supervisor.

"Buenos dias," Lillian calls sweetly from the partly opened bathroom door. She keeps Pickwick out of sight behind the door.

"Demonios!" the supervisor says under her breath. Then her voice takes on a polite tone. "Sorry. I will come back later." She dashes from the room. Lillian wonders why she came at all, quite sure that the woman would not do cleaning herself.

"Things get more curious every moment, Pickwick. I think we are going to catch ourselves a thief."

⸎

At exactly ten o'clock, Harold, with Lillian, and Pickwick at her side, waves for José and asks to go to the Joyeria de Ricardo [hoy-er-ee-ah day Ree carrd o], one of the fanciest jewellery stores in town. José checks with his dispatcher, and they set off.

"It's my wife's birthday, and we've decided to choose a gold necklace to remember the occasion." José seems as excited as his passengers when he drops them off at the joyeria.

"Come back at eleven, José. We should be able to choose something by then," she says.

Forty-five minutes later José arrives at the store for Harold and Lillian. She clutches a handsome blue Ricardo's shopping bag with something inside of it the size of a book. While they drive back to the hotel, Lillian pulls a velvet box from the blue Ricardo bag. She opens it with the back of the lid towards the front seat to hide its contents from José. Quietly, Lillian and Harold ooh and ah over their new purchase without letting José see what they have in the box. After a few minutes, she closes the velvet box and returns it to the blue shopping bag. Next, Harold and Lillian have a quiet conversation—quiet, but loud enough to be sure that José can overhear snatches of it.

Harold starts the whispering. "That's very valuable my dear. We must put it in the hotel safe."

"We haven't time, Harold. You have that luncheon with the mayor, and I have a hair appointment at that shop next to the hotel. It will be fine for an hour until my hair is done. My appointment is not until eleven thirty. I have time to take it to the room now. You must ask José to keep right on driving, or you'll not get to the mayor's luncheon by twelve noon."

At the hotel, with the blue package clutched to her bosom, Lillian leaves the taxi with Pickwick. They make their way through the revolving doors. Harold asks José to drive on to the mayor's official residence.

"Por favor, señor, may I slip into the hotel for a moment and use the washroom?"

Harold waits. He is quite sure that José is using the time to call his "dispatcher" in private.

When José returns, he drives directly to the mayor's residence with no dispatcher call.

How did Lillian guess that would happen? Harold asks himself. He knows that driving to the mayor's home will take until noon and marvels at his wife's planning.

Lillian goes to their room and continues with her plan to catch the thief. She places the blue package on the bureau next to the TV and partially conceals it with her sun hat. She goes to the sliding glass doors to check that the wooden bar is down, locking the doors, and that the drapes are open so that anyone on the balcony would be able to see the blue Ricardo's shopping bag. Next she takes another white plastic bag and polishes its surfaces. She places a previous purchase in the bag and casually leans the bag against the glass doors—a bag that will have to be moved to lift the wooden bar, a bag that will carry fingerprints if it is moved. Then she takes Pickwick's bed into the bathroom.

"You can sleep there if you like, Pickwick. For the next hour you and I are going to sit in here quiet as cockroaches and listen for whatever might happen." She adjusts the door until it is only open a slit—a slit that gives her keener hearing.

At twenty minutes to twelve, the door lock clicks. A person tiptoes to the sliding doors, the white plastic bag rattles, and the wooden bar gives a little "Plunk" against the window. The person leaves and relocks the door. Pickwick whines to be let free to sniff about, but Lillian cuddles and shushes him into compliance.

Ten minutes later Lillian hears the sliding door. Yes, she is right. The first person lifted the wooden bar so a second person could enter from the balcony. The glass door slides open, and a person enters. Lillian smells heavy perspiration. Pickwick smells it too. She holds Pickwick's muzzle closed to keep him quiet.

Footsteps move towards the TV, the blue plastic bag rattles, and the thief retreats to the glass doors.

"Alto ahi [Al-to ah-ee]!" shouts a voice on the balcony. It's the plainclothes policeman, shouting "Stop where you are," guesses Lillian.

Pickwick is beside himself with the indignity of being held by the muzzle. He works free of Lillian's grasp, scratches at the slightly open bathroom door, and rushes into the room with a barrage of harsh barking to confront everyone he sees.

"Caramba!" It is Miguel's voice, caught between the policeman and Pickwick's fierce protection of his territory. Lillian comes from the bathroom to stand by Pickwick and block the hall door in case the thief dares to pass her dog.

The blue shopping bag falls to the floor. The catch on the velvet box releases. The box is empty—meant only to lure the greedy thieves into the open. The policeman quickly has Miguel in handcuffs.

"When I shouted 'alto,'" says the policeman to Lillian, "this fellow was backing out of the sliding doors. He was trying to fit the bent end of this wire into the little hole across the end of the wooden bar so he could direct the bar to drop into place again as the glass door closed. I must take the velvet box and this stiff wire for evidence."

"Take that white plastic bag at the window as well, officer. It will have the fingerprints of the third person in the thievery ring."

Lillian has the policeman phone the officer waiting for Harold at the mayor's residence. He is to arrest José when he and Harold arrive and take them to police headquarters.

Before leaving the hotel with Miguel, Lillian explains to the plainclothesman that she is sure the housekeeping supervisor, Maria, is involved as well, and the four of them, with Pickwick, drive to the station.

⊷

Detective Paredes invites Lillian, Harold, Rosalia and Pickwick into his office.

"Lillian, you have singlehandedly broken a thievery ring that has troubled that hotel for some time. You managed a three-way trap and caught them red-handed. How did you know it was the three of them and not just one thief?"

Lillian considers her answer, for there are so many little details that caught her attention from the day they first arrived that thoughts whirl in her head. She sits and thinks.

First José—obviously he picks the travelers he wants to befriend, those going to the Paraiso Hotel with green tags; plus, why would he have two dispatchers? One time he referred to his dispatcher as "he" and one time as "she." Next there was the way Pickwick sniffed a path to the sliding doors that first time I thought I smelled heavy perspiration in the room and later when he growled at Miguel. It had to mean something. Now, with Miguel in handcuffs, that bit of the puzzle was solved.

Next, the cellphones. Each of her suspects had a phone. Even Miguel, despite his lower position as a gardener, had one. Would the hotel give Miguel a cellphone for "hotel business," like he said?

Lillian continues to organize her thoughts while Detective Paredes waits.

Yes, it was the stiff steel wire in Miguel's tool barrel that jabbed my hand when I stubbed my toe—not a usual gardening tool—and the little hole in the sliding door's wooden bar that put it all together. It was José's job to look for a good mark among deplaning passengers. When he drove hotel guests to some engagement, his "dispatcher" phone calls alerted the thief as to when it was safe for a theft to take place. This meant that there were at least these two in the thievery ring.

But the housekeeping supervisor, how does she fit in? Lillian smiles to herself. *"Damn dog" indeed. If Maria is part of the ring, Miguel must have just called on his cellphone to say he won't rob a room with that fierce dog in it.* That would account for the anger in her voice, followed by her oath towards Pickwick. She had just blistered Miguel on her cellphone before their encounter in the hallway—told him she'd make trouble for him with management if he didn't do his part in their thievery ring, dog or no dog. This meant that Maria was part of the ring, but again, what part did she play in the thefts? Of course—she had the keys to all of the rooms. Her job was to lift the wooden bar out of the way so the sliding door could be opened from the outside.

Lillian continues to consider her thoughts on Maria for a few seconds. *At first I couldn't prove it was Maria who lifted the bar, but many of her actions and her accusation of Rosalia certainly pointed that way. Now, the fingerprints on that white shopping bag placed over the bar will have to be the proof. She likely lifted the wooden bar, then phoned Miguel to go into action. With potted geraniums on the balcony, it was quite logical that he might climb up the short distance and tend the potted flowers. What a nice little routine they had.*

Lillian raises her eyes and looks squarely at Detective Paredes. "How did I know that there were three in the thievery ring, you ask? When you are blind, you notice many things. Rosalia's story about her family plus logic told me that Rosalia was an honest person, and I wanted to see her go free. Perhaps I put all the clues together, talked it over with Pickwick, and came up with a theory that you and I tested together. Thank you for giving my plan a chance to prove Rosalia's innocence. You have made my Mexican holiday a grand success." And for some unknown reason, Pickwick held up his paw to "shake a paw" with Detective Paredes.

BUNGLE-ITIS

IV

Lillian and Pickwick, her black lab guide dog, make their way past stores in Foothills Shopping Centre. Heat from the summer sun reflects off the sidewalk and burns against the soles of her feet, protected only by her white sandals. She pushes at her thick steel-grey hair for relief from the heat and humidity. Lillian hears people passing on either side of her and wonders why they would choose to shop in such unabating hot weather. Of course, she rationalizes, today she has a cheque she must cash. That's different. She doesn't have a choice.

Freshly baked bread, sniffs Lillian as she passes through the delightful aroma wafting from the bakery.

"Pickwick, straight—one more entrance to reach the bank and cool all six of our footsies." Lillian knows that Pickwick doesn't understand any of her extra comments, but it gets lonely inside her head, and Pickwick is a good listener. She cannot wait to escape the heat of the day by passing through the two sets of double doors into the bank's air-conditioned interior. Pickwick leads her through the people dominating the sidewalk.

When Pickwick pauses, Lillian pushes at the door beside her. It swings open, and she starts to take the four paces that will bring her to the second set of doors.

"You can't go in there," barks the voice of a young man. "The bank's closed."

"And why is that? It's one thirty on a Wednesday afternoon. It should be open."

Pickwick is not impressed or deterred by the young man's security guard uniform. He walks around him to lead Lillian to the second set of doors. She gives the door a shove and leaves the young man stuttering, "Bu-u-t, but ma'am, hey, ma'am," and without even a pause, Lillian and Pickwick enter the bank. With ecstasy, Lillian drinks in the cool air and walks sedately forward towards the cashiers' counter to stand behind a person already at the wicket.

The bank is as quiet as a tomb.

"Why is it so quiet in here?" Lillian says to the room in general, hoping that someone will answer.

"How'd you get in here?" snaps the voice of the man in front of her.

Hearing such a disagreeable sound to his voice, Lillian decides to politely chide him. "Through the door. How else?" She pauses, then adds, "I can't hear the clerks working. What's going on here, anyway?"

"God, you're thick, lady. A bank robbery, what else? Now shut up and get over there with the others sitting on the floor!" Something jabs at Lillian's arm. She wonders if it is a gun.

Because she can't see if he has a gun and because she is annoyed with the man ordering her about, Lillian's cussed side decides to present itself. Blindness has never stopped her tongue.

"Not so fast, Mr. Bank Robber," says Lillian in her most contrary voice. "No doubt you are pointing where you wish me to go. Because I am blind, I can't see which direction that is, and I have no intention of sitting on the floor." She continues to stand directly behind him. Pickwick sits in front of her just to the left of the man's heels and glares at him with his "don't-hassle-me" steadfast eyes.

As Lillian can't see terror across the faces of the employees huddled on the floor, she doesn't feel the fear expected of her. Lillian decides to spout inane comments to see if she can make this bully lose focus when faced with someone who insists on being amiable.

"Tell me, is your gun black or silver?"

"What's it to you? I told you to shut up."

From his sharp comeback to her question about the colour of the gun, Lillian is sure that he does indeed hold a gun.

"All the others can see the gun. They know what it looks like. I've never been in a bank holdup before. Because I'm blind, I need you to tell me a few of the details so I can enjoy the suspense a bit better. Tell me, Mr. Bank Robber, why do you rob banks? There must be an easier way to make a living."

"How would you know, standing there with diamonds on your fingers?"

Lillian holds up her left hand as if admiring her rings and admonishes the man in a superior fashion. "If I had to earn a living, rather than rob banks I think I would start a school for bank robbers. I'm sure I could figure out a heist to the last detail. I bet you don't even know where the bathroom is."

The man grunts as if she has raised thoughts of the possible need of one. Lillian can tell that her absurd remarks are getting to him. She decides he deserves to be harassed. She will ask if he gave his wife rings.

"Hey, X!" comes a shout from behind the cashiers' counter. Lillian considers that she may now think of Mr. Bank Robber as Mr. X.

The voice adds, "I can't get the cash cage open. It must have an automatic locking device that took over when we ordered that bank dame outta here. I've been trying to pick the lock, but it's taking too long."

"You've got a crowbar," says X. "Use it, and hurry up. Just because we stopped the dame from pushing the alarm doesn't mean the cops aren't gonna show up. Someone outside might get suspicious and call them."

The man at the cash cage starts to pound metal on metal and swear. Lillian considers this to be her cue.

"Ah yes, now I hear him. You have a partner who wants into the cash cage so he can scoop up the money. What's he going to put it in, smelly gym bags? No, that's wrong, but I've guessed that you're all dressed in uniforms like security guards. That would be the best reason why the man at the door thought I would have enough sense to stop when he blurted 'Stop.' You plan to wheel the money out of here on a little bank dolly—right onto the street and into a waiting grey security van."

She senses the man turning away and immediately feels for the back of his head or side of his face to see if he's wearing a mask.

"Geez, lady! You just about got yourself popped between the eyes. I don't want to kill nobody, so just stay out of my hair."

"Oh, I didn't want to feel your hair. I wanted to know if you were wearing a nylon stocking over your face or a wool balaclava. From the feel of it, my guess is a balaclava. Am I right? The weather is really far too hot to be wearing winter

53

headgear. Does your balaclava go with the rest of your outfit? You can see my pale-yellow slacks and shirt. The others know if you are colour-coordinated, so why shouldn't I know?"

"Stay out of my hair! Out of my hair, lady!" he shouts. "Don't ya know what that means?"

"Yup. I'm just trying to give you a bad time. You are bad, you know."

Lillian hears another voice.

"Hey, Ed. Do ya want me to waste that dame? She's driving me crazy."

The voice is younger than the voice of Mr. X [whom she now knows as "Ed"], *but it has the same tone—maybe a younger brother,* thinks Lillian.

"Now ya used my name, twerp," says Ed. "I told ya you're too young to keep cool on this job. Just keep your gun trained on those bank clerks, and let me deal with this blind nutcase."

Lillian counts aloud. "There's Doorman, Twerp, Ed, and Crowbar. My, my, four men to rob one bank. That's not very good planning. Too many crooks. They'll all want some of the lettuce when you divide up the loot. Just think, each of you could have hit a bank of your own and had more dough to spend on some cute ta-may-ta."

"You're asking for it, lady. Go sit down, and shut up," screams Ed.

Aha, he's losing face in front of his gang. His yelling is pathetic.

"No. I'm going to wait right here behind you so I'm first in line after you've gone. I really need to get this cheque cashed today."

The man grabs her arm and gives her a shove to the right. "There's a chair. Go sit in it. Sit, or I'll bust your kneecaps!"

Lillian is quite pleased with the way the man is losing his cool, but with Twerp so anxious to use his gun, Lillian fears he might unload it into Pickwick. She knows the direction of the information desk and pretends to wander a little until she reaches it, rather than the chair that Ed likely intended. She sits in the chair behind the desk and, for his protection, urges Pickwick to sit in the desk's kneehole with drawers on either side of him. The cold, smooth surface of the desk tells her it is made of metal. Pickwick will be less at risk.

"And keep your hands where I can see them," shouts Ed.

Lillian does as she is told. This must please Ed, to see her comply for once, and make him feel he is again in control. "Keep your eye on the bunch of them, Twerp, while I see why Double X is taking so long at the cash cage."

Lillian decides it's time to bug Twerp.

"Twerp—that can't be your name. Do you like being called Twerp?"

"Ed told you to shut up," shouts Twerp.

From the sound of his remark, Lillian knows that Twerp has turned his head in her direction to speak.

"No, no. Don't look over here, Twerp, or the bank camera will get a perfect front view of your face. The police will be able to identify you."

Hoping that Twerp is sufficiently dimwitted to believe her remark, Lillian counts on him to swing around and face the people on the floor again. She quietly lifts the phone on the information desk from its hook, lays it on the desk in front of her, and punches in 9-1-1.

When she hears a voice answer she starts up with her own conversation.

"Now listen to me, Twerp. Listen very carefully, and maybe you'll get the message. You're young, and I hope you're bright enough to copy what I'm saying." Twerp shuffles his feet. *Good,* thinks Lillian, *I must be bothering him. He thinks I'm talking for his benefit.* Lillian does her best to emphasize the important words.

"Why have you hooked up with these *other three bank robbers?* They can't be too smart if they think they're going to make much on this *heist. Foothills Mall* may have a bank, but there are bigger banks than this to rob. Just think: with *the alarm system still off* you've had lots of time to get the money. You don't need Ed. You could do this on your own with that *security guard uniform* and all. It's not as if *the bank clerks have given you any trouble, sitting there on the floor facing your gun."* Lillian knows some of her comments don't quite make sense, but at least they may be passing on the intended information.

Twerp hasn't come over, thinks Lillian, *so he can't have seen that I have the phone off the hook. He must still be looking towards the bank clerks on the floor. Poor boy, he doesn't realize that cameras will have his picture from the other corners of the room. What's even more stupid, he's likely wearing a hot balaclava and hasn't enough sense to figure out that the cameras won't get much of a picture.*

She knows that she may be only six metres away from him in case he loses his cool and tries to shoot her, but she decides to take the risk and unravel him as much as possible.

"Nice shoes, Twerp. Have they got bright colours on them? New treads? If you step in oil or hot asphalt in the parking lot, I bet the soles of your shoes will leave nice prints. You really should wear shoes with no tread for robbing banks."

"Gawd, lady, someone should cut out your tongue."

Lillian is delighted with his reaction.

"How old are you? Just out of kindergarten? Why, I bet you've never fired a gun in your life. What do you say? Have you practised on a firing range?"

Bang!

Glass tinkles as a picture on the wall behind Lillian crashes to the floor. She hears one of the bank clerks giggle. Another one whispers, "Poor Queenie got it right in the chops." Lillian slips the phone receiver back on its cradle in case someone comes over to inspect the bullet hole in the wall.

Ed gallops from the cash cage. Lillian does her best to slide down in the chair behind items on the desk. "Who's shooting? Are the cops here?" The room is dead silent. "Damn. That was you, Twerp, wasn't it? I never should have loaded your gun. It's a good thing we have the cash on the dolly." Ed turns to face the bank clerks sitting on the floor. "All right, you guys—over on your bellies, and don't move, or Twerp here—" Ed's voice turns sarcastic, "may actually be able to hit you in the butt at that close range."

Open eyes attract attention, thinks Lillian. She closes her eyelids like a Greek statue and tries to look as lifeless as Methuselah in his 970th year, with the hope that Ed has forgotten she exists. Her brain ponders the situation: *911 has had all the time they're getting. Let's hope the police figure out my message. I can't think of any more information I could have given them—number of robbers, guns, security guard uniforms, bank address, no alarm turned in—why, I even got Twerp to fire a round into the wall in case the bullet matches up with some other robbery.* She hears the bank robbers' footsteps crossing the floor. *Not enough time for the police—they're going to escape.*

"Get with it, Double X. Why so slow?" shouts Ed.

"One of the wheels on the dolly keeps seizing up. I'm almost dragging the thing." Lillian can hear the slight squeak. *Too heavily loaded,* she thinks, but she doesn't dare move a muscle, let alone make more remarks.

Heat blows in from the street. *They've opened the door. Where are the police? Maybe they think my message was a hoax and aren't coming. I sure wish I could open one of these eyes and sneak a peek.* She listens. They are between the doors about to leave.

"Hands up!"

The police? How did they sneak up like that? I didn't hear them. Feet scrape this way and that between the two sets of doors. Swearing and police commands carry in on the air. The scuffling of shoes ceases. *Have the police rounded up the bank robbers?* she wonders. People are moving on the other side of the bank. Someone is approaching. Lillian waits for the person to speak.

"Great job, ma'am!" Lillian realizes that a policeman is addressing her. "We copied your message and followed all your tips. We came without screaming sirens and snuck into position outside the street doors. We wanted to catch them between the doors when they were leaving. We couldn't risk a gun fight on the street, and we didn't want any of you in here to be taken hostage."

Lillian can tell from the sound of movement in the bank that the clerks are on their feet and coming her way. She sits still, cheque in hand, and hopes that despite their ordeal, one of them will cash it.

The policeman speaks again.

"How did you manage to stay so cool?"

Cool? First Lillian thinks of the pleasurable air-conditioning; then her thoughts turn to Ed, Twerp, Doorman, and Crowbar and her moments of personal amusement derived from this absurd encounter. She smiles, stands up, and brings forth Pickwick in harness from his place of protection under the desk. Attempting a most serious countenance, she says, "It was easy, officer. I'm blind. I wasn't afraid, because I couldn't see their guns, but I could hear the fear in their voices, so I tried to rattle them."

"Blind? You're blind," says the officer, then he laughs as he says, "Maybe we should hire blind cops. You and your dog gave these guys such a dose of bungle-itis, you foiled the heist."

RAW COURAGE

V

"Oh, Pickwick," Lillian exclaims to her black lab guide dog, "isn't it nice to be out walking again without snow? Surely you appreciate spring as much as I do!" Lillian can't wait for warmer weather so she doesn't have to wear her grey hoodie and fleece pants. "A few more steps, Pickwick, and we'll be back on our street and headed for home."

Lillian passes the corner house. She's been told that the flowering almond is in bloom, that it smells like orange blossoms, but she finds the perfume very faint. She runs her left hand along the fringed branches of Lionel Gibson's cotoneaster hedge. The buds are still small. Next comes the home of her neighbour Maria Petryk. Maria doesn't grow any shrubs that Lillian can smell or feel.

She hears someone crash through the hedge that grows along the side of Lionel Gibson's lot, separating his house from the Petryks' house.

"Who's there? What's happening? Are you all right?" calls Lillian.

"It's only me—Lionel. I think I see smoke coming from the basement window of the Petryks' house. I burst through the hedge to check. Can you smell smoke?"

Lillian turns her head towards the house and sniffs the air.

"Yes!" shouts Lillian. "I smell it. If you can see it, you'd better call 911."

Lillian hears Lionel crash through his hedge again. Boots pound up steps. His front door opens with a click, and he cries out, "Sarah, phone 911; the Petryks' house is on fire!"

Lillian hears him come through the hedge again, this time with his hose turned on full blast. He heads away from her down the side of Petryks' house. She stands as if bolted to the ground, not sure what to do. She hears the Petryks' front door bang open, stumbling footsteps, and coughing. Smoke swirls heavy in the air.

"Maria, is that you?" Lillian calls. "Did you just collapse on the lawn?" Lillian urges Pickwick forward towards the coughing. She hears three-year-old Naomi crying. *They both sound like they're on the lawn. Maria must have carried their little girl from the burning house.* "Straight, Pickwick, to-wards the crying." Pickwick moves onto the grass towards the child and mother. When he stops, Lillian bends down to touch the coughing woman.

Roused by the touch, the woman cries, "My baby, my baby!" and she tries to rise.

"Where is your baby, Maria?" Lillian demands in a voice loud enough to get through to the befuddled woman. Lionel hears the question and comes running, still carrying the hose. Lillian senses that more neighbours have been attracted to the scene.

"Maria, where is little Tommy?" Lillian asks again.

Maria's eyes open wide. She coughs and wails, "In the back bedroom, asleep in his crib!"

Immediately, Lillian rips off her hoodie, then puts it on backwards and pulls the hood up over her face. "Quick, someone pull the strings of the hoodie and make the face opening small to cover my hair. Lionel, douse my head with water."

"You're going after the baby?" asks Lionel. "What are you thinking, Lillian? You can't see."

"Right, Lionel. I can't see with the hoodie on frontwards, either. I know this bungalow from morning coffee visits. Its L-shaped hall goes down to the bedrooms. I don't have to see. I just need protection from the smoke. Make my head wet and lead me to the front steps!" After such a command, Lionel turns the hose on Lillian.

"Here, someone standing on the sidewalk, hold my dog's harness. Stay, Pickwick. Stay! Now someone lead me to the front steps. The firemen might take too long getting here to save that baby. Do as I say! I know what I'm doing."

With Lillian's commands, someone takes her arm, walks her forward, and places her hand on the railing of the front steps. In a moment, Lillian has climbed the four steps and disappeared into the cloud of smoke. Her hand reaches through the smoke and pulls the door shut behind her.

Lillian takes three paces forward with her right hand rubbing along the wall that's across from the arch leading to the living room, all the while forcing herself to think of the best way to save the baby.

The smoke will be less if I crawl on the floor. On hands and knees she turns right at the hall corner and continues to crawl along, with her shoulder rubbing the wall on her right.

Oooh, the floor is getting hot to the touch. Too hot for my hands and knees. She stands but crouches low.

I hear flames crackling in the basement. The wooden stairs are on fire. The door to the basement must be open!

She moves across the hallway, reaches out with her left hand to find the edge of the basement door, and flings it shut. She feels the left wall of the hall for the linen cupboard, passes it, and rushes into the next doorway.

The crib should be in here. She slams the door behind her, stands erect, and feels her way around the room. She bumps into the change table, kicks a wastepaper can, and runs into a chest of drawers. Finally, she feels the rungs on the side of the crib. Her hands pounce upon the quiet form. She grasps blankets and baby to her bosom. With one hand outstretched she directs her feet towards where she thinks she'll find the door.

Here it is! The door handle's hot. The fire must be worse. Gotta hurry. She yanks the door open and breathes heavy smoke. She coughs. *My hoodie must be dry. With this much smoke, I daren't return along the hall to the front door.*

In two strides she crosses the hall to the master bedroom. She turns to her left and walks forward until her shins hit the bed. She bends low and dumps the listless child onto the centre of the bed, reverses direction, and returns to the doorway.

The bathroom's right here at the end of the hall, and my hoodie's dry from the heat. I mustn't collapse from smoke inhalation. She struggles with a second fit of coughing as she enters the bathroom. Lillian grabs a towel in passing the sink, kicks the toilet, and steps into the bathtub. She cranks on the water and shifts the lever for the shower. Water pours over her head and shoulders. She holds up the towel to soak it as well and then rushes back to the bedroom. She feels for the quiet little body and lays the wet towel over him.

Shut the door. Throw the pillows at the crack under the door to stop the smoke. Find the window. It should be over to my right from the end of the bed. She cracks her knee on an upright chair, then finds a desk and reaches above it. There is the window. She pounds on the window with her hand, but with the commotion she hears outside she knows they'll never hear her pounding or see her in the smoke.

"Gotta break the window," she mumbles. She pounds it with a book. *Need something sharp.* In desperation she grabs at the air to find the chair she'd knocked over. She turns from the desk and flails her hands down around her knees to find the chair.

"Gotcha!" Now disoriented, she takes hold of the back of the chair and swings it in a circle until it crashes against something. She reaches out to touch a wall and moves along with one hand rubbing at the wall, feeling for the window, while the other hand drags the chair behind her.

Drapes. The window is next. "Ouch!" She catches the corner of the desk in her groin and crunches forward in pain. *Forget it, Lillian. Swing the chair. Swing it as hard as you can. Hit the glass with a sharp leg.*

Bang!

I don't hear glass tinkling. Hit it again. She swings with the force of an Amazon.

I heard a crack. Something drops on the floor. She feels the chair. *So it's lost a leg; the chair's our only chance. Why doesn't the window break? Why is the baby so quiet? Please, God, I have to save that baby before the smoke gets to me. Swing it again, hard!*

Crash! Lillian sucks at a gush of fresh air through the wet hoodie.

I'm through! Swing again and again. Make the hole bigger. There's Pickwick barking. He's right under the window! He knows I'm up here. Voices out there are calling to me. The fire engine's siren just stopped—it's here! She puts her hand up to the window and waves it about to determine the size of the hole.

"Oooh!" *I've cut my hand, but the hole's big enough for the baby.* She walks away from the window, bangs her shins on the bed again, and scoops up the baby and the blankets and wet towel.

She reverses direction towards the commotion she hears outside. The desk is in the way. She puts her knee up on the desk, and then, without knowing exactly how she did it, she finds she's kneeling on the desk with the baby in her arms. Urged on by Pickwick's barking, she thrusts the baby through the hole in the glass.

"We're here below," shouts a man's voice. "Drop the baby; we'll catch him. *Drop the baby!*"

Although her thoughts are clouding, Lillian drops her bundle.

"We've got him! Good work! Now climb out yourself and be quick about it. The roof's gonna cave in!"

Lillian can hear the firemen shouting to each other, fire hoses gushing, glass tinkling. She cringes from the stench of the burning house. The Petryks' cat screeches past her and flies out the window.

He said climb out. How do I climb out, and where will I land? She coughs. Her knees sag. *Gotta climb out, but how big is the hole?* She remembers that somehow she climbed onto the desk. A fresh breath of air helps her to think. *Reach down for the windowsill, kick at the shards of glass.* She pulls her cuffs over her hands and feels for the windowsill down around her knees. *Yes, there's glass shards. Many voices below. Gotta stand… kick…hole…big enough. Pickwick's barking for me to hurry. Gotta stand and kick out gl—*

Succumbing to the smoke, her knees sag, and she falls through the hole in the glass.

◦❧◦

"Where am I?" she cries out. A warm nose nuzzles her hand. "Pickwick, you're here!" She feels oxygen puffing at her nose. A hand touches her brow.

"You're in an ambulance, Lillian. I'm an E.M.S. You had a fall and a lot of smoke, but you'll be okay once we've stitched up your hand, checked you for bruises and concussion, and turned your hoodie around." He laughs. "You and your dog are heroes. You saved the baby boy by minutes. He had just about succumbed to the smoke. It was your dog's barking and breaking loose to run to that window that made the firemen realize you were pounding on the window in all that smoke. In seconds, you broke through that multi-paned window like a gorilla trashing his compound, with flying glass everywhere, produced the baby, and fell out the window yourself."

"I did all that? I just wanted to save the baby." Lillian holds Pickwick's paw. "Thanks for barking, Pickwick. You always know where I am."

"Woof."

COMPUTER GEEK

VI

In the front hall of her home, Lillian fastens the harness on her black lab guide dog. When she is sure it is in place she calls upstairs to her husband. "Pickwick and I are going for our morning walk, Harold. Do you want to come with us?"

It is Saturday—a summer day bright with sunshine and blooming flowers. The perfume of purple petunias growing near the front porch wafts through the screen door. Lillian is sure Harold will say yes.

"You go on ahead, Lillian. I have to finish this letter and post it at the mall. I'll walk over. If we time it right, I can meet you on Alpine Street and describe the neighbours' flower gardens to you." He knows that the Alpine Street route takes his wife close to an hour to complete.

"Fine, Harold. See you later."

Lillian and Pickwick step onto the front porch, feel the glorious warmth of the sun, and set out on their walk. Pickwick leads Lillian around something on the driveway. Curious to know why the dog took the little detour, she doubles back. Her foot finds that the hose and sprinkler have been left at the front door. *Harold was likely watering the petunias last night,* she thinks, and she turns Pickwick towards the route that will lead them home via Alpine Street.

They pass through patches of sun and shade and past the scent of Mrs. Bamber's honeysuckle bush. With the sweet smell of a fresh-cut lawn and the sound of garden clippers at the Neufelds' house, she calls a cheery "Hello" to Abe, who loves to be outside tending his garden.

Pickwick knows the route well and needs no direction as they make their way along the familiar streets. When they round the corner that Lillian knows to be Alpine Street, she listens to her watch.

"Pickwick, do you see Harold up ahead? Forty-five minutes should have been enough time for him to finish his letter and post it. He said he would try to meet us here." Pickwick sits when he hears Lillian's voice and starts walking again when he feels pressure on the harness.

Lillian walks along at her usual pace, waiting to feel some reaction on the handle of Pickwick's harness. She enjoys talking to her dog and is quite sure he understands her conversations.

"You haven't urged me to hurry. That means you don't see Harold, do you, Pickwick? Oh well, plans don't always work out. Maybe he's still at the mall."

Lillian and Pickwick turn at the driveway of her white stucco home with the Dutch-blue shutters. She climbs the two steps onto the front porch and proceeds to fit her key into the door lock. To her amazement the door pushes open. *Harold must be home,* she thinks.

"You beat me home, Harold."

She hears him upstairs in the computer room. He does not answer.

"You missed a lovely walk," Lillian calls up the stairs. Still Harold does not seem to hear her. Lillian moves away from the sweet smell of petunias towards the hall closet where she keeps Pickwick's harness. She notices the smell of cigarettes in the hallway—the kind of odour imparted by the clothes of a smoker. *Where did that come from?* she asks herself. *Harold is allergic to cigarette smoke.* She jokingly calls the house a "no-smoke-er-dope" zone.

Pickwick seems uneasy.

Perhaps that's not Harold upstairs. Maybe I've trapped an intruder, she thinks. She clips Pickwick's soft leash to his collar so he can't race upstairs and confront whoever is there. He might get shot. If it's Harold, taking precautions won't matter.

Lillian moves closer to the staircase and shouts, "If that's an intruder up there, you might as well know I'm blind. You can race down the stairs and out the front door, and I won't see a thing. Go on, leave!"

Nothing happens. Lillian is not surprised. She has shouted these words many times before and always been wrong, but somehow shouting out at the empty house makes her feel better.

Perhaps the door pushed open because Harold wasn't sure if I had my key, she decides.

Across from the foot of the staircase are glass-paned French doors leading into the living room. The double glass doors are always kept closed as a signal to Lillian that everything in the room has been left in its proper place by the last of the family to leave the room so she doesn't trip on the footstool or knock a glass from the coffee table. Nothing is left out of place in their home. Habit causes Lillian to reach out to touch the doors as she turns towards the kitchen.

Her hand moves sideways into space. The doors are open! She knows Pickwick would have reacted if someone were there standing in the room. She smells more of the lingering cigarette odour. Her heart pounds; she knows for sure that an intruder has been in the living room. If he's still in the house, why didn't he run when she gave him the chance? She gathers in Pickwick's leash to hold him close, and together they walk silently to the back of the house and the kitchen phone.

Again, she pauses to listen. Everything is quiet. Is she imagining trouble? Perhaps. She tells herself to calm down. Harold will soon be home. Thirsty from her walk, she decides to settle her nerves with a glass of iced tea.

In that moment of quiet before pulling at the refrigerator door, her sensitive ears catch the quiet click of their laptop being opened directly above her in the computer room. No. She is not wrong! Someone is up there.

Her head swims for a moment. *Quick, Lillian,* she tells herself, *make a plan—think of something to do besides running away. You're safer in here where you know where everything is. Outside, you would be vulnerable. Besides, you can't run away. You never run—you can't see, remember?*

If he didn't leave when he had the chance, he must have a reason for staying. Maybe he's searching through our software files, but what would he be looking for? I let him know that I heard him. In order to phone 9-1-1 without arousing his suspicion, I must speak to him again—cause him to think I don't know he's an intruder. But what can I say?

She calls up the stairs, "Harold, you are just like an absent-minded professor the way you can get so intent on what you are doing. I suppose you're still working on that letter. I'm going to pour me a glass of iced tea. I'll pour one for you—cookies, too, if you want them, but you'll have to come and get them."

Lillian wishes she had her cordless phone but knows it is upstairs beside her bed. She picks up the kitchen phone to phone 9-1-1 but stops herself. The wall phone is too close to the front hall. Her voice will carry up the stairs. If she is listening for him, he must certainly be listening for her. She must pretend to have someone to talk to.

Then Lillian thinks of Harold. She wants to stay near the door to warn him not to come in. *Why, that's it—lock him out! He's so macho he might go upstairs and confront the person and get beaten or pistol-whipped or whatever it is intruders do.*

Lillian walks to the front door and silently opens it. She pushes the doorbell, lets the screen door slap shut, and slips the catch to lock it.

"Why, Mr. Pickwick, how nice of you to call," she says to her imaginary guest. "Harold told me that you had moved in across the street. Will you have some iced tea with me?" Lillian leads Pickwick back to the kitchen.

"Right this way, Mr. Pickwick. We can sit at the kitchen table. Harold tells me the living room is dull at this time of day, and I can feel the sun lighting up the kitchen. I'll pour a glass of iced tea for you." She brings out the lowest range of her voice and gruffly mutters, "Fine, iced tea, fine." Anyone sitting at the kitchen table would not be seen from the front hall. Lillian places three glasses of iced tea and a plate of cookies on the table.

"Have a cookie, Mr. Pickwick." Pickwick is confused. He cocks his head and looks at the tempting morsels but knows he is not allowed "people" food.

Lillian seats herself on the stool at the kitchen wall phone. She starts a conversation to disguise the dialling of 9-1-1. She doesn't care if the intruder hears her well, but at least he must think she is talking to a visitor and not on the phone.

"It's nice to see you fixing up the place across the street," she says. Pickwick blinks his eyes, unsure of the meaning of her words. A voice answers the phone call and wants her to designate police, fire, paramedics, or poison control.

"Police," she says crisply, then adds, "were around your house when it was empty."

"What's that?" the voice on the other end of the line demands. "I'm not sure I follow you."

"Yes, *the police.* One day I was quite sure I saw *someone nosing around.*" She had to think of more to say so he would trace the call to her number and determine her name and street address. "Of course I couldn't call over to see if you had moved in," she says to "Mr." Pickwick. "How could I *trace the number?*"

"You're not making any sense, ma'am. Is this a prank, or are you in trouble?"

"Yes, whenever *there's trouble,* I always say it's good to have people near at hand when you need them. I'm so glad that you and I are having this little visit."

The policeman speaks again. "Yeah, lady, we're having a visit all right, but I'm not quite sure what it is that you want. Is someone there, maybe listening to you, that isn't supposed to hear you call 9–1-1?"

"*How right you are, Mr. Pickwick. Now if there's anything you'd like to know* about the district, *you just ask me questions, and I'll be glad to answer.*"

Now and then Lillian tries to add a grunt or clear her throat in an attempt to sound like a comment from Mr. Pickwick. Pickwick senses Lillian's troubled voice and sits alert at her feet.

The police officer speaks again. "I'm guessing you think there is an intruder in your house. I'm having your number traced now, so stay on the line, and the police will get there soon."

"*That's so nice of you* to say so, Mr. Pickwick. *I'll try to keep in touch. When did you say your brothers will arrive?*"

Just then Lillian hears the board on the upstairs landing squeak.

"*Oh my goodness, I think my upstairs guest is moving around.*" Then she cups the phone with her hand and hopes he hears her whisper, "Because I'm blind, I feel much wiser when I hear everything. I'll try to stay in touch, but I have to go closer, and I can't take the phone with me." She leaves it dangling on the cord.

Lillian creeps to the hall doorway to hear if the top stair creaks as well, to know if he is coming down. *It's a good thing I didn't let Harold repair the stairs. Those squeaks are a very useful part of my communication system,* comes flooding through Lillian's thoughts.

There is no second squeak. Her ears tell her that the intruder has gone across the landing into their bedroom. What's he searching for? *He won't get jewellery—it's not in there. Harold's filing cabinet? What if he's searching through my drawers and mixes everything up?*

Lillian finds her dander rising. She feels that the intruder is taking advantage of her blindness—taking his time, searching where he has no business to be. It's one thing to think he can steal the computer, but search the bedroom? He has violated her space, and that truly annoys her. *No more Mrs. Blind Nice Gal,* she decides. *I'm going to make his life just as miserable as he's making mine.*

She takes the chance of walking around the house at will. If he is listening, he can think she's doing housework. A plan starts to form in her mind.

The stairs, I have to block the stairs or make them difficult to descend. She quietly places a seat cushion from the sofa across the three bottom stairs. It doesn't cover enough stairs, so she gets a second seat cushion and places it above the first. *Too obvious,* she thinks. She tosses the throw cushions onto the seat cushions and covers the whole lumpy area with the living room afghan. *There, if he's carrying away our things, that should give him something to think about.*

The angrier she feels, the more cantankerous she becomes. *I hope he tries to jump to the lower landing and breaks his ankle.* To increase the odds of that happening, Lillian goes to her grandson's living room toy box and feels for pull-toys that have wheels. She places these below the cushions on the landing where the stairs turn for the final singular step into to the hall.

As she makes more sounds, so does the intruder. Lillian hears the drawer of the filing case slide open. This infuriates her even more. She brings the mop and broom and jams them between the spindles of the railing so that the handles obstruct the higher steps. The railing! With all of those obstructions, he'll have to steady himself with the railing.

Lillian grabs the cooking oil from the kitchen and dribbles it on the golden-oak handrail as far up as she can reach. She smears it over with her hand to make sure it is totally slippery, then runs her hand around the top of the newel post and on the doorknob of the screen door.

What next? she thinks as she washes the oil from her hands. She is quite determined to continue making things worse as long as the thief takes advantage of her. *The hose—*

Harold left it right at the front door. If that miserable cuss up-stairs makes it out the door, he'll have to run through the hose if I can turn it on. Lillian, with Pickwick, sneaks out the kitchen door and feels her way along the outside of the house until she comes to the hose bib. She turns it on full blast.

When she returns to the kitchen she hears the landing squeak again. She leads Pickwick into the hall closet, where they hide, quiet as scorpions. This time the top step squeaks.

"Jeez, lady, are you mad? What's all this crap on the stairs?"

It's the thief—swearing at her. *Right, you stupid geek, I'm mad,* she thinks from her hiding place. *Mad at you! Now go ahead, lose your balance, and grab for the railing.*

Something hard hits the wall of the staircase. A guttural scream cuts the air, followed by a string of cuss words and the sound of a body falling down stairs.

Lillian listens. *He's getting up. Too bad. I guess he didn't break his neck.* She hears him gathering the things he dropped.

"Damn, she put oil on the doorknob too," he screams. "And locked the door! What a nutcase. If she was here, I'd belt her one." Lillian hears him trying to work the catch on the screen door.

Belt me one, seethes Lillian. *Whose house does he think this is? Oh, how I'd love to see fear in your eyes.* Oblivious to danger and totally vindictive, she ruffles her short steel-grey hair into peaks to look as witchy as possible, takes a firm hold on Pick-wick's leash, and bangs open the closet door. Landing with her feet astride and her free hand pointed like a gun, with all her might she screams, "*Hands up! I gotcha.*"

For a second there is complete silence. Lillian imagines him with mouth open, gawking at her. Pickwick growls and barks. He strains at the leash, his front paws lashing forward, his teeth bared, ready to devour the intruder.

"Keep that damn dog off me!"

Lillian hears the man scrabbling to work the lock on the screen door.

Why should I? "Get him, Pickwick," she shouts to make the dog appear to be a trained guard dog while she lets the leash out a little to frighten the thief into thinking the dog is charging at him.

The door catch clicks. The thief yells, "And the hose too. What a crazy ol' bat." He races through the sprinkler and down the street.

From the other direction, within a moment, Harold arrives at their driveway. He stops short when confronted with the sprinkler and wonders why a dishevelled Lillian is standing at the doorway pumping an exultant fist in the air.

"Why are you so happy?" he shouts.

"We had an intruder. He made me angry coming in here and then staying to search upstairs even longer when he thought I was defenceless. I showed him. Maybe I didn't catch him, but I bet he never comes back, 'cause I made his life miserable when he was trying to get away."

A police cruiser screeches to a stop in front of the house. An officer jumps from the passenger door.

"As we came around the corner, we saw this fellow trying to run down the street. He could hardly see where he was going with water droplets on his glasses, and his clothes were all spotted with water. Now why would a guy carrying a laptop computer run through a hose, we asked ourselves? So we nabbed him. Is this the intruder that was in your house, ma'am?"

"Likely, if he's wet," chuckles Lillian. "I'm blind, I didn't see him, but I made sure that my dog, Pickwick, did. You'll have to ask him."

LITTLE JENNIFER

VII

The smell of salt air and the quiet rush of waves as they spread over sand and recede tell Lillian that their one-month summer vacation on Quadra Island will be a huge success. She holds her face to the sun and instantly wants to know every corner of the property so that Pickwick, her black lab guide dog, will recognize the gardens and how to cross the sandy beach to the water's edge.

"Come, Lillian, take my hand," says Harold, her husband. "I can see there is a bench close to the seaside. We'll walk it together so Pickwick will know the route across the sand and be able to take you down there anytime you wish."

She counts the paces as they go. Seagulls squeal overhead. The sound of each wave becomes more distinct. Harold's running commentary tells her to expect some small boulders littering the sand and that the sea is very blue, with three sailboats in the bay. He also talks about a big black tanker forging ahead on the horizon. When he stops walking, Lillian stops counting—one hundred and three paces, she notes.

"The bench is over here, Lillian—off to the right." After ten paces, Harold pats the seat of the bench, Pickwick sits opposite from where Harold has indicated, and Lillian sits on the bench, facing out to the sea. A soft breeze ruffles her steel-grey hair. Lillian fills her lungs with the humid salt air in complete contentment as memories of growing up beside the sea in Blackpool flood through her head. Harold sits beside her, still holding her hand, and shares her moment of pleasure.

"The bench is about three metres long," says Harold, "so it shouldn't be hard for Pickwick to stop where you can feel for the back of it and find the seat. You are about fifteen paces from the water, but it could be closer or farther away depending on the tide. Let's go back and have a walk around the patio and front flower gardens. Then we really must go in and organize lunch."

❦

By three thirty in the afternoon, Lillian decides she wants to return to the seaside.

"Pickwick and I are walking down to that bench again, Harold. We'll be back in a little while." Absorbed in a book, Harold sits in the sunroom that faces the back patio. He grunts in recognition of her comment, and she leaves by the hall door that opens towards the ocean.

They cross the flagstone patio. Before stepping onto the sand, Lillian removes her sandals. She loves the feel of warm sand on her feet and wet sand between her toes. As Pickwick leads the way, Lillian wonders if the tide has changed the watermark. At least with bare feet she will know when she is getting too close to the water.

Pickwick leads Lillian straight for one hundred paces, then stops. After some urging, he goes towards the bench, but she feels certain he has something on his mind. Finally he sits. Lillian feels for the bench, turns, and makes herself comfortable on it. Pickwick does not come closer to sit at her feet.

"Hello. Is there someone nearby? I'm blind, so please speak up. I wouldn't mind a visit with someone." Only the sound of the waves washing up on the sand can be heard. "I really think someone is sitting on the bench with me. Please speak to me."

The voice of a child answers.

"I'm sorry if I'm using your bench, Mrs. I didn't think anyone was in your cottage, so I've been coming here to listen to the sea. Don't be angry with me."

"Angry? Far from it! I'm delighted. Would you like to pat my dog?" Through vibrations in the bench Lillian feels the child move closer. "Just a minute while I take off his harness and put on his leash. He's a guide dog for the blind, and people aren't supposed to pat him while he's in harness. Once I clip the leash to his collar he will feel much better about the attention of a stranger. There, come and pat him on his shoulders. My name is Lillian, and his name is Pickwick. What's your name?"

"Jennifer," the small voice answers.

"Jennifer is a pretty name. You sound like you are about ten years old. Am I right?"

"Mm-hmm," is all she says, but Lillian takes it for a "yes." It seems like conversation only continues when Lillian asks questions while the child strokes Pickwick's back.

"If you like the ocean so much, can you swim?" asks Lillian.

"No," says the child.

"Do you have a pet?"

"No."

The little girl seems very shy. Lillian decides her questions must be designed to avoid yes-and-no answers.

"My eyes can't see anything," she explains to Jennifer. "Perhaps you can make my day prettier if you tell me what you see." Lillian asks if there are popcorn clouds in the sky, the colour of the waves, and if there are any freighters on the horizon or fishing boats in the bay. With each answer the child has a stronger voice and seems happier to be talking to this strange woman who sees with a dog.

The child startles. "What's that noise I just heard?"

"That's my watch," says Lillian. "I wanted to know if it was four o'clock yet. The watch speaks out and tells me the time when I push this button. I'll push it again for you—listen."

In a metallic monotone, the watch says, "Four-o-five."

"It's after four already? My mother will be home soon. I have to go or she will be mad at me. Maybe I'll come tomorrow," says Jennifer, and Lillian hears her running down the beach without another word.

The next day Lillian returns to the bench at three o'clock. She wonders if Jennifer will arrive. At three thirty she hears the crunch of footsteps on the sand, and Jennifer's voice says, "I've come again. May I sit on your bench with you?"

"Why of course. Pickwick and I have been waiting for you." Lillian wonders why the child is so reticent to assume she is welcome. Perhaps her parents are very strict and it's hard for her to know her place. Whatever the cause, Lillian enjoys the sweetness of the little girl and wants to know more about her, but she decides that they should talk about boats in the bay and the seagulls until she feels Jennifer is more relaxed. Jennifer reports that without any wind, there are no sailboats.

They talk about a fishing trawler making its way down the coast and the gulls before Lillian steers their conversation around to talking about themselves.

"You can see that I'm old enough to be your grandma, with my grey hair and thick glasses. What colour is your hair? Is it long or short?" Answering a series of questions, Jennifer describes herself as having brown hair and ugly freckles.

"Mother cut my hair short after Daddy died because she doesn't have time to brush it into ringlets now that she has to work. He died when I was in grade one." Then Jennifer adds, "Grandma died last year. She lived with us, and I miss her."

Lillian decides she had better change direction in their conversation, but just as she is about to start a new subject, the little girl fidgets.

"Is it four o'clock yet?" she asks.

Lillian plays her watch—four-o-two—and again Jennifer leaves for home. Lillian decides that the child has learned to sense the passage of time and fidgets when her mental clock warns her that she must return home.

The next day, Lillian, quite taken with the little girl, goes to the bench at ten minutes to three. Jennifer arrives at five to three, and they begin their visiting anew. Jennifer describes the brown-and-white long-legged sandpipers strutting on the beach. She says her mother cooks at a nearby restaurant, but when asked what her father used to do, she falls silent.

"Where are your friends? I hear children calling to each other as they ride their bicycles past our cottage on the front road."

"I can't go bicycling," Jennifer blurts out. Her voice grows strangely quiet as she adds, "My new stepfather rides my bike to work every day. He's a mechanic with dirty hands. He works in that garage way down the road."

81

That's new, thinks Lillian. *She's never mentioned having a stepfather before.*

"Who is with you all day if both your parents are working?"

"Nobody, now that Grandma's dead, but it's okay. I can look after myself."

When four o'clock passes, the child runs for home. Lillian realizes the child is troubled—lonely, not too pleased with her stepfather, and somewhat afraid of her mother.

Many of the stories of each day have become dinner conversations with Harold. They determine that they can't do much to help the child but to listen and be friendly.

The next day Lillian asks Jennifer if she would like to come for lunch the following day. The child declines, saying that her mother wants her to stay home, out of trouble, and clean the house, and her stepfather expects her to have supper ready. Lillian is even more dismayed. She wonders if times will be more difficult for Jennifer when tourism declines in the fall and money becomes a household issue.

"If you are supposed to stay home, how is it that you can visit with me every day?"

The little girl doesn't answer at first. Lillian can hear the child squirming on the bench. "M-mmy…Umm…Mom-my…Umm…" Jennifer doesn't seem to be able to finish the sentence. Lillian waits. Finally, the child moves a little closer, ready to share her secret.

"I don't like my stepfather very much. He comes home at three, has a beer, and then acts kinda funny, so I come here until Mom comes home at four. When I see her coming down the sidewalk, I sneak in the back door. Most days John doesn't know I'm not there. He likely thinks I'm reading outside in my hidey-hole under the back porch. He's too fat to climb in there." Lillian determines that "John" must be Jennifer's stepfather.

⁓

"So that's her story, Harold. The home is not a happy place, and it isn't fair that Jennifer is caught in the middle of it all. I suppose life was bearable as long as her mother worked and her grandma kept house, but now that's all changed, and I can't think of anything we can do about it."

⁓

The next day Jennifer does not come; nor does she come the day after that. On the third day Jennifer walks quietly down the beach at three thirty, one slow step after another. She sits at the far end of the bench, convulsed with barely audible sobs.

"What's happened, Jennifer? Why are you crying? Are you hurt? Unhappy?" There are no answers to any of the questions. Lillian tries to put her arm around Jennifer to comfort her, but the child draws away.

Pickwick, free of his harness and clipped to his leash, rises from the sand and sits quietly at Jennifer's feet with his head on her lap, but she continues to sob quietly, unable or unwilling to form any words.

Suddenly, she stands. "I'm going wading now. Goodbye," she says, and she walks away towards the water.

What a strange thing to say, thinks Lillian—*just like that—"I'm going wading now."*

"But you can't swim! What if the tide catches you?" cries Lillian, trying to focus her sightless eyes on the back of the child. She hears splashing. Jennifer has entered the water.

She listens for what seems a long time. Nothing. "Jennifer, are you out there? Answer if you can hear me," but all Lillian hears are soft waves washing onto the sand and receding.

Maybe Jennifer has waded along the beach out of hearing, she thinks. Then Lillian, holding only the dog's leash instead of his harness, walks towards the water until her feet feel the wet sand. With ears trained to hear what her eyes cannot see, she listens. She thinks she hears someone calling.

"Help! Help!" comes floating on the soft breeze. Yes, someone is definitely shouting for help. It sounds like a child. With thoughts of her youth when she could see and took a course in lifesaving, Lillian prays that she will be able to find the child in time. Without a moment's hesitation, she tugs on Pickwick's leash, crashes into the frigid water, and wades with giant strides.

The water gets deeper. Pickwick bounds through the waves beside her on the end of his leash.

"Pickwick, can you see her?" The dog wades deeper and starts to swim. Both Lillian and Pickwick are strong swimmers. Pickwick always enjoys their winter vacation in Mexico, where they swim together.

Again, Lillian hears the cry for help. She corrects her direction and fights the tide towards the cry. Pickwick thrashes on ahead.

Lillian struggles to make speed against the deepening water. She clips the end of the leash under the belt of her shorts so she and Pickwick can swim together far out from shore. She hears another cry for help, weaker but closer.

Pickwick tugs on the leash, leading Lillian on. She is slapped by waves she cannot see. She prays that Pickwick will see her and the person calling for help safely home from this vast, confusing vortex of rising and falling waves.

Pickwick starts to bark.

"Where are you Jennifer? Call out so I can find you," shouts Lillian. No response. Pickwick tugs on the leash and barks again.

"Where, Pickwick? Where do you want me to go? Oh God, if you could only give me sight for a moment," she screams. "Jennifer, please call out!"

You're losing your cool, Lillian, she says to herself. *Pay attention to your senses.*

Pickwick tugs again. Lillian pulls hand over hand on the leash towards her dog. Pickwick drags her a little this way and that until Lillian feels a small torso just under the surface of the water. Quickly, she draws it to the surface. Is it Jennifer? Lillian feels for the child's hair. It is cut in a short bob. It must be Jennifer!

All Lillian's lifesaving techniques from her youth in Blackpool flood her mind. She draws the little girl across her bosom where she can reach her mouth and nose and blows into the child's lungs as she pulls with her free arm and kicks out in a scissor kick. Trying to swim and perform mouth to mouth resuscitation every sixth count makes progress slow.

Lillian begins to tire, but still she continues trying to revive the child as she swims. The child coughs. Success!

"Pickwick, home. Swim for shore!" and together, Pickwick and Lillian with the flaccid little figure struggle with the waves as they swim towards the beach. The chill of the water and fighting the waves takes its toll on Lillian's strength.

With shallower water, Lillian regains her footing. Silently, she praises her dog's ability as he strains on his leash to help lead his mistress onto their beach.

Without the support of the saltwater, the child becomes too heavy for Lillian, and she is forced to pull the little body by the shirt collar through the light surf until she reaches land. With her last dregs of energy, Lillian drags Jennifer well up the beach to reach warm dry sand, despite the child's plaintive whimpers.

Lillian unties Pickwick's leash from her belt. "Pickwick, get Harold. Go! Go home, Pickwick," she points. With his leash snapping on the sand, Pickwick races up the beach.

Lillian's lungs suck at the air. She drops to hers knees and wishes she could collapse, but the child seems so lifeless that Lillian knows there is more to do. She places her cheek near the child's mouth and nose to check for breath. *Thank goodness—she is still breathing, but so cold. Must try to warm her…take off her shorts and T-shirt and warm her in the hot sand,* she tells herself. Lillian feels for the shorts and finds jeans. She struggles to pull them off. Next, the T-shirt. She finds a long-sleeved shirt and rips at it in frustration. *Why is the child in slacks and a long-sleeved shirt in this hot weather?* she wonders.

꩜

Pickwick reaches the sliding doors of the sunroom. Without breaking stride, he jumps full length and crashes against the closed glass doors. He barks and races with little starts towards the beach, then returns to bark again. In seconds, Harold sees the loose leash and bounds down the beach after Pickwick.

Lillian has removed Jennifer's pants and shirt and covered the semiconscious child in sand warmed by the sun. From time to time, Jennifer bleats as if in pain.

Harold is soon beside them. He catches Pickwick's leash and hands it to Lillian, then picks up the child. The sand falls away.

"My God! She's all bruises. Her arms are blue, and so are her thighs," shrieks Harold.

"That must be why she was whimpering when I dragged her up on shore. I couldn't take the chance of falling with her in my arms. Bruises! I couldn't see them. Oh, Harold, do you think she wanted to drown herself when she first went into the water and then changed her mind? I can see now that she was trying to tell me that she came to the bench so her stepfather wouldn't find her and rape her. She likely didn't know the words to use, so she never told me the whole story—just snatches, like beer and her stepfather coming home an hour before her mother. No wonder she didn't like his dirty hands."

Harold holds Jennifer gently across his arms as they walk up the beach towards the cottage. The child rouses, sees that her long-sleeved shirt and jeans have been removed, her secret unveiled. Her countenance crumples in a look of terror, and she utters a fresh scream of agony.

"Now, now Jennifer, everything is going to be okay," says Lillian. Harold places Jennifer in a sun lounge on the patio, then runs to get a blanket. Lillian kneels beside the sun lounge and holds the little girl close to contain the child's wrenching sobs. "Don't worry, Jennifer, your stepfather will never touch you again,"

Lillian coos over and over.

Harold returns with two blankets and a cellphone. "Hello. Please send the paramedics to 1387 Beach Road. We've rescued a child from the ocean. And bring a social worker with you. The little girl will need her." They wrap Jennifer in a blanket, and Lillian cuddles her while they wait for help to arrive. Gently, Harold places the second blanket over Lillian's soaking-wet clothing.

Pickwick makes two trips down to the ocean. First he brings back the little girl's clothes. Next he returns with his harness. Finally, he sits at Lillian's knees, close to Jennifer, and stands guard with large soulful eyes while the approaching sirens that are screaming in the distance grow louder, then abruptly cease.

The paramedics and the social worker take over, but Lillian and Pickwick know that they have a new friend.

THE ADVENT CANDLE

VIII

Lillian stands at the mantel feeling the length of her advent candle, set firmly in the cool brass candlestick holder. It's a Christmas candle meant to be burned down a little at a time on each of the twenty-five days before Christmas, and she knows it's not the same as the big advent candle at church, but she still likes to call it her advent candle. She cannot see the flame that burns brightly each night when Harold lights the candle at dinner, but she can feel the heat it offers, and this has become one of her Christmas traditions. Each evening after dinner, Harold replaces the candle on the mantel where Lillian can find it. This morning her fingers tell her that the candle is finally very short.

"Today is Christmas Eve, Harold. I'd love to go to the early evening service when they sing half an hour of carols before church starts."

"I knew you'd want to go, Lillian. I've already looked it up on last week's church bulletin. That service starts at 7 p.m. I think of all the special days at church, you enjoy this one the most."

They both turn to last-minute jobs dictated by the Christmas season.

❦

The stove bell rings. Lillian takes the last batch of cookies from the oven, and the glorious aroma of fresh shortbread floats through the house. Harold comes into the kitchen.

"I've just hung the last bobble on the tree, Lillian. The house looks ready for Christmas guests, and the smell of that shortbread is the finishing touch. We'll have a whole afternoon to catch our breath before church this evening and Christmas Day."

"You must have put spruce boughs over the living room archway, Harold. I can smell them as well as the shortbread. I'm sure the house looks lovely. Come, it's time for lunch, and then we can have our naps."

❦

The phone rings. Lillian awakens and rolls over to reach for the bedside phone. "It's for you, Harold. I think it's Jack, the chairman of your outreach committee at church."

Harold takes the receiver. "Hello, Jack. Merry Christmas. What's on your mind? Really? That's too bad. How can I help?" The conversation leads to the need for paper and pencil. Harold moves off to his study to take notes.

Lillian rises, makes afternoon tea for them, and sets a plate of shortbread cookies on the table in the breakfast nook. Pickwick, Lillian's black lab guide dog, joins them for his doggie treat.

"You were right, Lillian. That was Jack on the phone. I'm afraid you're not going to like what I have to say."

Lillian sighs. Harold goes on. "You know that new country church group that our church adopted for part of our outreach program? Well, Jack and his wife were supposed to drive out there tonight, but both of them are in bed with the flu. The committee has collected our older hymnbooks for them as a Christmas gift to the new congregation. They meet in their local community hall. It's a little hard to find, especially in the dark. Anyway, the children have written their own nativity pageant and are putting it on this evening. They weren't going to have refreshments, so Jack offered to bring a chocolate slab cake. He doesn't want to disappoint them. I'm the only other person on the committee who's been out there and knows the way. Jack asked us to fill in for them. What could I say?"

"I bet you said 'yes.' I'll just have to sing carols out there. When do we have to leave?" Her words are bright, but Harold sees a touch of disappointment on her face. He suspects she is quietly thinking of their own church service that she will miss.

Harold casts his eyes upward to the kitchen clock and muses out loud. "It is already four o'clock. The children's program starts at seven, and the drive should take an hour, but to be sure let's say an hour and a half because it will get dark and we'll have to buy gas before we leave. I'd say we should leave by five. Can we be ready to go in an hour?"

"Sure. I'll pack a lunch and fix a thermos of tea," says Lillian, "while you pick up the cake and the hymnbooks and buy gas. That should save a little time."

Once Lillian has made the tea, she makes three sandwiches, fixes dog food and bottled water for Pickwick, and then decides she needs the cooler. She moves her hands along the basement shelves until she feels the smooth plastic cooler, and she takes it upstairs.

"The cake will look nicer on a tablecloth," she mutters to herself. She often talks to herself when the house is empty. Hearing her voice helps to keep her company. She moves into the dining room. "I'll just fold up our red-and-green plaid Christmas cloth from the dining room table. Harold tells me it has gold threads running through it. Oh yes, a knife to cut the cake, and a stack of Christmas napkins for plates." She pauses. Her eyebrows pucker. "My advent candle—we won't be here to light it." Without another thought, Lillian retrieves the advent candle, including its brass holder, and places matches and the candle in the cooler.

Harold is not home yet.

Lillian's mind keeps churning. "I don't want to be out in the country with no way to stay warm if we run into bad roads." She piles three blankets, one each, in the back hall, ready to go into the car, then she goes to the bedroom to put on her heavy red sweater and comb her thick greying hair.

෧෨

Harold returns. They load Pickwick and the cooler into the car and set out on their drive to the country. Harold always comments on the passing interests during any drive.

"The first part of the trip is on the main highway, Lillian. It's dry. We won't have any trouble along here. I listened to the forecast. It isn't supposed to snow, but they said the wind might pick up. But you never know; if there's wind there could be snow, too. We'll just have to take our chances."

When they turn onto the narrower side road, Harold pulls over to lift the sandwiches and cookies from the cooler in the back seat. Lillian pours two mugs of tea. The rural countryside is very quiet. While they drive along, finishing their supper, Lillian imagines soft white flakes of snow decorating spruce trees along each side of the road, even though it is already dark. She can't see the headlights carving two shafts of light into the moonless night with poplars and country bush crowding in on each side of the road. Although they are eating the only "dinner" they will have, she realizes that it is no time to burn the advent candle. *Maybe when we're back home,* she thinks.

At the next intersection, Harold knows he must turn left.

"Whoa! Get a load of that wind. The bush back there was protecting us, and now we're driving right into it. I'll have to slow down. The wind is whipping so much snow into the headlights, I can hardly see the road."

Lillian hears the car go into second gear and hears the wind whistling in the side mirror. She senses by his silence that Harold is tense at the steering wheel. She listens to her watch; it's 6:30.

"How much farther is it, Harold? The program starts in half an hour."

"Don't worry. If I don't get stuck in drifting snow, we should be there by seven. I'd rather get there at the last moment than take the car out of second gear."

Time seems to drag. The car seems to drag. She knows that Harold is concentrating on his driving and that it is not the time for conversation. Blackness crowding in upon her brain makes Lillian feel very isolated. She puts her hand into the back seat and gives Pickwick a friendly pat.

At first he nuzzles her hand. Then he leaps up to the window with sharp barks. Harold stops the car and looks in the direction of Pickwick's eyes.

"There are the lights of the community hall," Harold yells. "I would have driven right past it with all this snow in the headlights if it hadn't been for Pickwick. Good dog! And seven o'clock on the dot."

It is ten minutes after seven by the time they manoeuvre through the snow into the parking lot, attach Pickwick's guide dog harness, and arrive at the hall door with the hymnbooks, slab cake, and cooler, which holds the tablecloth and Pickwick's dinner. Wind and snow rush into the hall when the door is opened.

"Come in, folks, come in. Ooh. The wind is really picking up. Where are Jack and his wife? I thought they were coming. You're Harold, aren't you? We just started with one carol and a prayer. The children are all in the wings offstage about to begin their idea of a nativity pageant."

Harold introduces Lillian and Pickwick to their greeter. They take seats at the back of the room. From the sound of the teenage emcee's voice introducing the children's play, Lillian figures that there are only about four rows of seats in front of her. The room is cold. She leaves her coat on. The rustle of nylon winter jackets all through the audience reminds Lillian that community halls seldom start up the heat until folks arrive. Everyone's coat is rustling—about thirty people, she decides.

"Shhh. They've begun," Harold whispers to Lillian. "The stage has no curtain, no props so far. A boy in a striped bathrobe and bandana, Arab style, has walked onto the stage leading a live donkey. No wonder they didn't want to hold up the kids' presentation. I wonder how they got the donkey onto the stage. Mary is walking beside the boy in a white bathrobe and a pale blue headscarf. She has a huge pillow in her tummy."

Lillian doesn't hear any dialogue for this scene, but the donkey's hooves clip-clop around in a circle on the stage, and then the noise goes into the wings.

"The lights have flicked off," says Harold. "With no curtain for the stage, I guess they plan to turn the lights off to change scenes. They're on again. Now the stage has two bales of straw, I suppose to look like rocks or clumps of grass. A shepherd is sitting on one bale, and a second shepherd is standing. The kids have wooden staffs, head scarves, and darker robes cinched at the belt. You'd laugh, Lillian. They have two live sheep on stage with them that look very bored."

"Ba-aa-a-a." Everyone snickers. Lillian wonders if the sheep practised her lines. Then, from a young voice, she hears, "Look, a star!"

Harold chuckles, then continues his monologue. "A white sheet just arrived, flapping its arms like wings. It must be the angel of the Lord."

Lillian hears Gabriel call out in a loud convincing voice, "Don't be afraid, guys. I've got good news for everybody. Tonight is very special. Tonight in Bethlehem years ago a baby was born to Joseph and Mary. They called him Jesus, the Saviour, so that's why we have Christmas." Lillian hears bare heels in a rapid sequence of little thumps as their owner retreats from the stage.

Lillian chuckles. "Gabriel must have departed without finishing his lines."

Then one of the shepherds says, "Gabriel, that angel who just left, told us we should find a manger with a newborn babe and worship him."

"The lights just flicked again, Lillian. The shepherds are gone, and the straw bales are piled to look like a hotel desk at the left side of the stage. Two kids in coloured sheets and headscarves are behind the makeshift desk. Joseph, Mary, and the donkey are standing in front it. The donkey is having a chaw at the straw in the top bale. It looks like the innkeeper is about to speak."

"Sorry, folks; baby or no baby, there is no room in the inn. Maybe you can find a warm spot out in the barn." The donkey's hooves trace a tattoo across the stage to the wings as before.

Lillian hears bare feet scurrying around on the stage and figures that the lights must be out again while they set up the manger scene. *Funny,* she thinks, *the Bible moves from the inn to the manger, and somewhere along there Mary delivers a baby. I wonder if the kids thought of that! They seem to think of everything else these days.*

Harold starts his commentary again.

"The two bales of straw are centre stage now, Lillian. Joseph has the donkey with him to the left of the straw bales, and Mary is sitting on the straw at the other side holding a real, live baby. She's bouncing him up and down in her arms. It's likely her baby brother, and she's bouncing him out of habit. The baby has wide-open eyes and is staring out at the crowd—pretty cute. To the right, the shepherds are on their knees with their sheep. A boy with a little drum has just arrived—now a little girl with a chicken on a leash. I guess they had to have a part for everyone."

Lillian senses a pause. She decides that the lights are off and they are changing the scene. In the silence, she hears wind whipping around the building. Thoughts crowd into her head. A country blizzard…the roads will be filled with snowdrifts. At least the hall is warm now. She sniffs the air, which is becoming more pungent by the minute. Certainly the donkey, sheep, and chicken have created a realistic environment for a manger.

"Are the lights off or on, Harold? I don't hear anything."

"They are off, but a farm lantern is flickering for the star of Bethlehem, and by its light I can see three figures moving silently across the stage." For a moment, Harold is silent.

"Ah, the lights again, and we are back with Joseph and Mary in the barn waiting for the kings to arrive. One sheep needed a shovel, the donkey still thinks it's snack time, and the chicken wants to jump off the edge of the stage and hang itself."

Lillian thinks she can hear the sound of shoes on the stage.

"The pageant doesn't have kings, Lillian. Three kids have just arrived on stage. A tall boy is dressed in overalls with a Stetson cowboy hat, like a farmer. Beside him is a cute teenage girl in jeans with an apron. She's holding the hand of a little girl in a frilly pink dress. They are grouped to look like a family, and each one has a gift wrapped in colourful modern Christmas paper, tied with a bow. They're kneeling in front of the straw bales. In turn, they are placing their gifts on the floor in front of Mary and the baby Jesus. Now they are sitting back on their heels with bowed heads and praying hands. It is really very effective."

"It sounds wonderful, Harold. I'd say the kids are trying to show that believing is as important today as it was when Jesus was born."

The voice of the young emcee asks the audience for patience while they turn off the lights one last time so the children can move into position for a formal crèche scene suitable for the parents to take pictures.

Lillian hears a gasp; then a sudden hush comes over the crowd. No one moves. She can't guess if the lights are on or off.

A man shouts, "Why did you put the lights out again, Henry? Turn them on. The kids are ready to have their pictures taken."

"I've tried, but they won't come on. Maybe the storm outside has dropped a tree across the wires or blown a post down. I guess that's it—the end of our Christmas party."

Harold jumps for the flashlight kept in the cooler and shines the beam over the children on stage. The soft glow of light, instead of the strong room lights, casts a magical patina over the scene. Parents rush up to snap their pictures.

"Hey, Dad! I can't get the lantern going again. I think it's out of kerosene."

An elderly woman's voice wails, "Without lights I can't play for the carols that we were going to sing."

"I'm sorry about the lights, folks," the first man's voice speaks into the dark." I guess there's not much we can do but go home."

Before the crowd begins to react in the darkness, Lillian whispers, "Pickwick, straight. Take me up to the front of the room." Then in a strong voice she calls out to the crowd, "Just a moment, folks. You can't see me in the dark, but I'm Lillian, from your sister church in the city. My husband, Harold, and I have brought you some hymnbooks and a large chocolate cake. Perhaps the lights will come on again if we wait a bit. I'm blind, so I don't need lights to play the piano. Please keep your seats."

There is a buzz through the room. Lillian hears a voice in the crowd remark, "What's she going to do? We can't read those hymnbooks in the dark."

"Harold, put my advent candle on a chair in the wings and be ready to put them centre stage after the first carol, and, ahh, would you mind leading the singing while you're up there?"

Harold smiles, though his wife can't see it. How can he say no?

Harold takes a hymnal and shines the flashlight on the index of first lines to find the section with Christmas carols.

Lillian continues to tell him her plan. "Look up 'Away in a Manger.' We'll sing it first while the children are on the stage. Shine the flashlight on them if you remember all the words. Face the audience and sing loudly so the folks can follow your lead. And don't sing many verses if they get lost when their memories can't help as much."

Harold marvels at how quickly Lillian can make a plan in the face of disaster. He taps the piano keys so Pickwick will know to lead Lillian to the piano bench, then climbs onto the stage and holds his flashlight as high as possible to shine on all of the children.

Lillian announces the carol "Away in a Manger" and strikes the opening chords for the hymn. A strong baritone voice lifts over the crowd, and everyone sings all three verses. Next, with the help of the flashlight, Harold has the children leave the stage and join their parents. The chicken goes into a cage, the two sheep flop down, and the donkey remains on its feet, tethered to the binder twine of one of the bales of straw, apparently asleep because of the dark. Harold gets the signal from Lillian to light the advent candle in the centre of the stage.

When everyone seems to be settled again, Lillian plays two chords on the piano, then rises from the piano bench.

"The little stub of candle on stage has burned down to one day before Christmas. I call this candle my advent candle. It would be wonderful if you would share it with me tonight by singing carols for a while."

The crowd grows quiet with the little candle as a focal point in the darkness. Harold announces the first carol offered in the hymnbook. As they go from one carol to the next, sometimes the people sing with gusto and other times a lesser-known carol sounds like a baritone solo. Still, Harold goes on in the dark, singing every carol with the hope that the lights will come on again before they come to the carol that Lillian always plays last.

"Hark the Herald Angels Sing" reverberates from the rafters, and "Good King Wenceslas" miraculously has a men's and ladies' arrangement as Harold leads them through the verses.

Lillian continues to play until they come to that last carol, and still no lights. *Serving chocolate cake in the dark is not going to be easy,* she chuckles to herself.

"Now, for our last carol," she says. "I'd like the children to sing the first verse alone because I'm sure they all know it—'Silent Night.'"

The voices of the children are so pure and innocent that emotion rises in Lillian's throat. Then the parents join in. Unknown to Lillian, her advent candle has sputtered and gone out during the last verse.

Again, she plays a chord for silence and then speaks into the darkness. "Thank you, everyone, for a wonderful evening. The pageant was perfect for our lives today, and you made me very happy to end Christmas Eve with my advent candle and Christmas carols. Harold and I will never forget this evening—"

At this point, before she can finish, there is a gasp, then a cheer. "The lights! They're back on again," someone shouts.

"And look at that huge slab of cake," shouts a teenager.

"And on a red Christmas tablecloth!" says a mom.

Then a kid says, "Hey, read the writing on the cake. It says, 'Happy Birthday Jesus.'" Everyone laughs.

"Oh, thank you, thank you," Lillian hears on all sides of her. "Thank you for coming."

"Thank you for the cake."

"Thank you for playing for us,"

"Thank you for bringing your advent candle."

Lillian wonders what kind of magic Harold managed in the last few seconds to have the tablecloth and cake set out for everyone to see.

A lady with a kindly voice says, "You and Harold were wonderful to drive out here with the possibility of blowing snow that's turned into a blizzard. The roads will be bad. You must stay with us tonight on the farm and share Christmas morning with our children."

Lillian has Pickwick lead her through the crowd to Harold's side.

"The wind has dropped a little, Harold, but the snowdrifts will be bad. A lady came to me and insists we stay the night and share Christmas with them on the farm. What could I say?"

"I bet you said 'yes.'" Harold mimics Lillian's answer from earlier in the day, and they both laugh.

The cake is devoured. The lay preacher calls everyone into a circle.

"Perhaps our visitors from the city would like to close with a prayer. Lillian, how about you?"

For a second Lillian panics. *The piano is one thing, but how do I lead a prayer? What will I say?* The prayer that they said at the close of Girl Guide meetings when a teenager springs into her mind. "Down" she says to Pickwick, who is standing patiently at her side, and he lies on the floor with his muzzle resting on outstretched paws.

"Look, Mommy, the doggy knows how to pray," says a tiny child.

Lillian bows her head and instantly decides to change the first five words of the poem to suit Christmas.

"On this special Christmas Eve, Father, hear our prayer, Bless and keep our dear ones safe beneath Thy care, Help us all to serve Thee, to be kind and true, And to keep a loving heart in all we say and do."

Everyone joins in with "Amen," and the room seems filled with the presence of peace as families collect their things and move towards the door with handshakes, hugs, kisses, and a chorus of folks calling "Merry Christmas!"

ABOUT THE AUTHOR

Lyn grew up in Winnipeg where her father, P.M. Abel, the editor of the Country Guide magazine, loved to amuse the family with stories. With her B.Sc. in Human Ecology and a post-graduate in dietetics completed, Lyn married petroleum engineer, Bill Thompson in 1953. They lived in most major oil towns and cities on the Canadian prairies, followed with postings in Peru, United States, England and The Middle East, when they enjoyed extensive world travel. They retired to Calgary where Lyn continues to live as a widow. No doubt Lyn's early upbringing is why we now find Lyn writing stories.

Lyn likes people and weaves the patterns of everyday life into her fiction and non-fiction. All her life she has been involved with serving, organizing, and managing volunteer committees for her community, including twenty-six years as a senior leader in the Guides and Scouts organizations. Sports included golf, downhill skiing, curling and swimming. Lyn has spent over sixty years enjoying their family cottage and all it has to offer in outdoor life, boating, and family togetherness, now with her four sons and their families.

Lyn has actively pursued the craft of writing for twenty-five years. Apart from serving on Writers' Guild of Alberta committees and the Executive, she has co-ordinated the Calgary WGA Prose Writers Critique Group for twenty-four years. In 2008 she was honoured with a WGA Life Membership. Lyn works in several genres but prefers to write short stories, novels, and her own style of poetry.

Her work includes *Hypothermia, Outhouse Memories and Other Cottage Poems, Bella A Woman of Courage 1863-1953* and three books of short stories–*Blind Justice, Children of the Thirties* and *Patchwork Stories.*

Visit Lyn at
www.lynthompson.com

CPSIA information can be obtained at www.ICGtesting.com
Printed in the USA
LVOW10s0812161214

418969LV00007B/102/P